From the Rise Universe

Volume 1

by

Mandy Collins-Moore

Rise (Rise, Book 1)

CM Stars Publications from CM Stars Creations

https://www.cmstarscreations.com/cm-stars-publications

Published 2023.

First edition published 2017. Second edition published 2023.

Contents

Dear Reader,

Some of you have been here before, in fact, for some of you, this adventure started seven years ago. So, why are we here again? The short answer is I felt a need to make things right. What does that mean exactly? When I originally released *Rise* and *Rise Mind Over Matter,* I was excited and so in love with the characters, and that never changed, but I was never truly happy with the way they had turned out. The formatting always bothered me, and I knew I could have worded so many things much better. Now, seven years later, I have decided to rectify those issues by releasing second editions of both books with new covers, new formatting, and some content tweaks. I felt it would be the perfect time to do so with the release of *Sandbox*, the next evolution in the Rise Universe.

Whether you're brand new to the universe or a veteran in the fight against the afflicted, I hope you find characters and themes you can connect with and feel for while enjoying the adventure. In addition, I also hope you know how much I appreciate each and every one of you who have been on this journey with me and who will hopefully embark on this journey with me in the future. Your support has meant the world to me.

You can pick up *Rise*, *Rise Mind Over Matter*, and *Sandbox* on Amazon or my website, cmstarscreations.com, and be on the lookout for the next expansion of the Rise Universe, *City of Hope*, coming in 2024. Until then, be good to yourself, be good to each other, and always reach for the stars!

Much Love and Hugs,
Mandy

ACKNOWLEDGEMENTS

A big thank you to Games4Kickz, Capp00, Gray-GhostZoro, Kage848, Starsnipe, JC's Channel, TexCub_SF, and Bearded Guys Gaming for agreeing to be part of this. You are all truly awesome humans and excellent examples of the wonderful people in the gaming community and the world in general. Your faith in me is more appreciated than you will ever know.

Thank you to all who welcomed me into the community and showed love and support for this series. There are entirely too many of you amazing folks to list, but you are each greatly appreciated. You will always have a special place in my heart.

My parents, Thomas and Peggy, what can I say? If it weren't for you, I'm honestly not sure I would have ever written my first story. You encouraged me and bought my first typewriter. I remember it very well, a Brother with built-in word processor. I loved that thing more than life itself, and I love you for all you did. Thank you, Mama and Daddy.

Last but far from least, my husband, Michael, and our kids, Chris, Amber, Jordan, and Desy. You may not know it, but each of you saved me in some way, gave me strength, and taught me valuable lessons. For reasons unknown to me, I was deemed worthy enough to be blessed with all of you. I didn't deserve you, but I am grateful for you every minute of every day. Thank you, my loves.

CHAPTER 1

The bearded man looked at his map once again before looking back to the street signs, obviously quite confused and frustrated. Glancing around the busy street and sidewalk he noticed a young man sitting alone at a table outside a coffee shop.

"Excuse me," he said in his thick accent as he approached the young man. "Sorry to disturb you, but I seem to be a bit lost."

The young man took a sip of his coffee before responding. "You're obviously not from here," he noted with a friendly smile.

"No, I'm from Ireland. I'm just visiting the States for a convention."

"Welcome to Arizona. Ireland, huh? I'm picking up a touch of an Irish accent, but I'm hearing something else in there too."

The bearded man chuckled. "Ah, very observant. Ireland by way of Germany actually. I moved to

Ireland several years ago. It makes for a funky accent."

"Not at all. It's kind of cool. Bet the ladies like it." The young man winked. "Anyway, I'll bet an Irish German lost in Roma, Arizona for a convention is looking for the Streamers and Creators Convention. Am I right?"

"Nice guess."

"You look familiar. I think I may have watched some of your stuff."

"My name is Jason Fran, but in the gaming world I'm known as Games4Kickz or just Kickz."

"Of course! Yeah, Kickz, I love your work," the young man enthused as he shook Kickz's hand. "Great to meet you! I'm David Star, but most folks call me Starsnipe or Star for short."

"I've seen some of your videos too. Great work!"

"Thank you, thank you. Well, I'm heading to the con myself. Stick with me, and we'll be there in no time."

Kickz grabbed himself a coffee and newspaper from the coffee shop before they set off toward the convention. The two top headlines on the front page of the paper were about the conflict most were predicting would lead to the third World War and a strange illness creeping across a few states.

"That stuff will rot your brain," Starsnipe quipped.

Kickz folded the paper and placed it in the

back pocket of his jeans. "Agreed."

During their short journey to the convention, they compared the two most popular platforms available for streamers and video content creators, Twitch and YouTube. Both had become wildly popular in recent years and were almost essential to many online personalities, not just gamers. Twitch afforded streamers the opportunity to interact in real time on a personal level with their audience while YouTube allowed creators to upload pre-recorded videos to their channels to keep their audience entertained and engaged. Kickz and Star discussed their experiences with both platforms as well as their general experiences as gamers, including some interesting stories about overzealous fans. They were enjoying their conversation so much they nearly passed their destination.

Kickz stopped in front of a large, brick building. "Is this it?"

"So it is. Shall we?"

"We shall."

The convention had rented out the entire building, and it was packed with streamers and creators along with fans hoping for a chance to meet their favorite streamer or creator or possibly get news about their favorite games. There was a sense of excitement and camaraderie in the air, but there was also a hint of rivalry between the pc players and console players.

"Times have changed," Star mused.

"Yes, they certainly have. I remember when people like us were considered losers who lived in our mothers' basements."

"We losers are having the last laugh, and we will laugh long, hard, and loud."

"Right now I have to laugh all the way to the bathroom," Kickz chuckled. "Coffee went straight through me. I'll be right back."

Kickz tossed his coffee cup into a nearby trash can as two young women who recognized Star approached him, giggling like a couple of schoolgirls. As Kickz headed toward the bathroom he couldn't stop himself from laughing. Times had indeed changed.

The man washing his hands at the men's room sink glanced in the mirror when Kickz entered the room. His eyes widened with recognition and excitement when he saw Kickz in the reflection. "You're Games4Kickz," he exclaimed as he quickly dried his hands.

The exclamation startled Kickz. "Uh, yes. That's what my wife writes in my underwear anyway."

"You've even got a great sense of humor in person, and that accent of yours is better in person," the man gushed, shaking Kickz's hand profusely. "My wife and I are big fans. To be honest, I think she has a little crush on you."

Kickz blushed. "I appreciate that. Thank you very much. It's always lovely to meet a viewer. Tell your wife I said hello."

"She's here too! I'll go get her. She's going to be so excited!"

"That's wonderful, but I'll meet the two of you outside. Somehow, I don't think she'd enjoy a smelly men's room."

"Good point. I'll be right back."

After the man left Kickz giggled before stepping up to a urinal. He relieved himself and had just begun to wash his hands when he heard retching coming from one of the stalls. It didn't sound normal. It sounded extremely painful. He looked under the stall door and saw the heels of a pair of brown tennis shoes.

"You okay in there," Kickz cautiously asked.

The only response was more retching followed by the toilet flushing. The stall door opened, and a tall, bald man dressed in a blood splattered shirt and jeans stumbled out and went to the sink. Steadying himself with one hand on the counter, he turned the water on and splashed his face. When he looked at himself in the mirror his reflection revealed to Kickz exactly how rough he looked.

"Been a rough day," he told Kickz when he noticed him watching.

Kickz tried to suppress the alarm he felt upon

seeing the man's condition. "Ja, looks like it. Are you going to be okay? Can I do anything or get anyone for you?"

"I think I should go back to my hotel room to lay down. It's just across the street," the man responded, his breathing clearly labored.

"I don't think you should walk alone. Let me help you," Kickz offered.

"Thanks," the sick man replied as Kickz took him by the arm to steady him. "I'm actually a fan of yours, Kickz. Wish I was meeting you under different circumstances. This is a little embarrassing. I'm Lou by the way."

"Well, Lou, it is very nice to meet you." Kickz started guiding Lou toward the door when he began to retch again. It sounded so painful Kickz winced. "Lou, maybe I should call for medical help."

Still retching, Lou shook his head. "Just need to lay down."

"Man, I really think..." Before Kickz could finish his thought Lou doubled over, threw his mouth open, and a large stream of dark blood emerged to splatter onto the floor. "Holy ballz! What did you eat? What is that? Did that come from that sketchy looking hot dog vendor I saw outside?"

Lou started to retch again. "Need to lay down."

"You need a doctor!"

Lou's friendly demeanor shifted. "I said no," he shouted in a growl.

He shoved Kickz against the wall with extraordinary strength. The impact was hard enough to take Kickz's breath and blur his vision. Lou ran from the bathroom making noises that sounded only half human.

Star was chatting with a few people when a commotion started near the bathrooms. A security guard was trying to calm a tall, bald gentleman who looked very ill and was behaving erratically. He lunged at bystanders, making strange sounds at them.

"Wonder what that's about," one of the men with Star stated.

"Probably some sort of stunt the convention set up," Star speculated.

"Sir, you don't look well," the security told the man. "Why don't you calm down, come with me, and let's get you some help."

The bald man slowly turned away from the gawking bystanders to face the guard who gasped when he saw the man's face. In a matter of a minute his appearance had deteriorated considerably. He looked more ill, his skin was an unnatural color, and a nasty sore had begun to form from his temple down his cheek.

"Sir, you're scaring everyone. I think you really could use a doctor. Come with me, and I'll get you help."

The man appeared to calm a bit. He quieted some as he slowly moved toward the guard. Then, without warning, he started to twitch in an abnormal manner and lunged at the guard, sinking his teeth into his neck. The guard managed to break free and tase him. People around them screamed and scattered.

A woman with Star giggled in amusement. "Pretty realistic stunt. They went all out this year."

"Almost too realistic," Star remarked with concern. "Maybe you guys should move to the exit just in case. I need to find my friend, excuse me."

Making his way through the frantic and screaming crowd, Star kept a watchful eye on the security guard and crazed man. To reach the men's restroom he had to pass within a couple of feet of them, and he wanted to be well aware of what they were doing. He was almost directly behind them when the guard tased the man again. It barely slowed him down. A voice asking what was happening came across the guard's handheld radio.

"I tased him, but the son of a bitch just keeps coming," the guard strained to say, all the while delivering another jolt to the man who simply stumbled backward before advancing on the guard again.

Star was amazed the guard could speak at all with the gapping bite wound on the side of his neck. Star picked up his pace and slipped into the men's room where he found a groggy Kickz sitting on the floor rubbing the back of his head. "Jesus, Kickz, what happened?"

"This big, bald guy was sick. When I tried to help he got pissed for whatever reason."

"I think he's still pissed," Star informed him as he helped him to his feet.

Kickz heard screaming from the other room. "What's happening?"

"I think your friend is pissed and crazy. He attacked a security guard, took a chunk right out of his neck. People are freaking out. Got a bad feeling about this whole thing."

"Perhaps we should leave?"

"My man, you read my mind."

Upon stepping out of the bathroom they discovered things had gotten horrifically worse. The guard was flat on his back on the floor with his crackling radio still in his hand. His eyes stared up at them blankly as Lou chewed on the intestines he'd pulled from the guard's belly. Star and Kickz jumped back and then realized Lou wasn't the only person indulging in a cannibalistic snack. One of the women Star spoke with earlier screamed as a group of people pulled at her and bit her. A man was holding someone's severed hand, eating the fingers as if they were appetizers. Kickz saw the enthusiastic fan from the bathroom gnawing on the arm of a woman Kickz assumed was the wife he'd told him about.

Star watched in disbelief as people trampled each other trying to get out. "We'll never get out of here. There's a bottleneck at the exit, and people are stepping all over each other to get out."

"We should try to get to the second floor. Maybe there's a fire escape up there. We definitely cannot stay here."

Star surveyed the room. "Over there!" He pointed to a door across the room. The sign above it indicated it led to the stairs.

Kickz evaluated the chaos unfolding between them and the door. He spotted a few folding, metal chairs leaning against a wall near them. Grabbing two and handing one to Star, he instructed Star to swing at anyone who tried to touch him.

"Don't worry, I have every intention of effing 'em up."

"Then let's do this."

The two of them began to work their way to the stairs by moving along the wall. They'd managed to make it most of the way to the door before Kickz's bathroom fan stepped in front of them, snarling and biting at the air.

"Oh, man, don't make me do this," Kickz pled.

"Please, move and let us be on our way."

Continuing to snarl, the man twisted his neck and titled his head in a freakish way.

"I don't think he has any idea what you're saying," Star observed.

Hearing Star speak agitated the man more. He snarled at Star and then reached for Kickz who instinctively swung his chair. The chair caught the man in the ribs and sent him flying backward, however, he never lost his footing. Kickz and Star were horrified to see him shake it off and charge at them. They both took aim. Star's chair connected with his kneecap, dropping him to the floor. A sickening crack emanated from the man's neck when Kickz landed a solid blow to it. To their surprise, neither blow deterred him as he dragged himself across the floor, occasionally reaching for them.

"Move," Star shouted.

They ran past the man and into the stairwell, slamming the door behind them.

"What the holy ballz was that," Kickz exclaimed.

"No idea, but I don't think we should stop moving."

They ran up a flight of stairs, coming to a landing where they discovered two men cannibalizing another man. One was chewing on his leg while the other plucked out his eye and devoured it. They were so engrossed in their meal they didn't notice Kickz and Star. Kickz mouthed to Star to go back down the stairs. When they made it back to the door they'd originally gone through they realized they could only go back into the room they'd escaped from or go down the stairs.

"I'm not going back in there," Kickz stated firmly.

Star looked over the stair railing. "Well, I don't want to either, but we don't know what's down there."

"I'd rather take my chances down there."

Star sighed. "Down it is."

The duo cautiously crept down the stairs, jumping with every noise they heard. At the bottom was another door that opened into a long hallway. As they moved down the hall, chairs raised and ready, they peeped into rooms in hopes of finding an exit out of the building. Midway down the hall they heard movement coming from a room just ahead of them. They approached it quietly. Suddenly a man holding a wooden broomstick emerged.

"Crap," the startled man yelled as he raised the broomstick.

"Who are you," Star demanded.

The man relaxed his stance. "You talk so, you must not be one of them. I assume your buddy isn't either then. I'm Pete." He lowered his broomstick. "You two creators, streamers, devs, or fans?"

"We're creators and streamers," Kickz answered.

"Your accent sounds familiar," Pete pointed out. After a momentary pause a look of recognition spread across his face. "Wait, you're Games4Kickz! Nice to meet ya, man."

"You too, I guess," Kickz hesitantly replied. "This is Starsnipe."

Pete smiled. "I've watched a lot of your videos. Nice to meet you too. I'm Pete Lewis, aka GrayGhostZoro or just Gray."

Kickz and Star finally lowered their chairs. "The circumstances are unusual to say the least, but nice to meet you too," Star replied.

"What did you mean by we weren't one of them," Kickz probed.

"One of those freaking psychos upstairs. I was in the main room when this bald guy went nuts, and then the guy next to me tried to bite me. I tried to get out the front exit, but people were just jammed up in the doorway and crushing each other." His voice trailed off as he recalled the gruesome scene. "What the hell is going on?"

"We're not sure," Star admitted. "What we are sure of is our best bet is to get out of this building and watch the news later to find out what happened."

"I'm not going back upstairs! Not a snowball's chance," Gray emphatically informed them.

"No, no, no. We're not even considering that as an option," Kickz assured him. "There has to be some other way out."

"Maybe each of us start checking rooms and doors," Gray suggested. "If one of us finds a way out we get the other two and get the hell outta Dodge. Otherwise, we meet right back here in say twenty minutes?"

Star shook his head. "No way. That is exactly how people die in horror movies. That's a large nope for me."

Gray snickered. "This isn't exactly a horror movie."

"I'd say that whole scene upstairs comes about as close as you can get. It qualifies," Star retorted.

"Okay, Star, what do you suggest then," Kickz inquired.

"We stick together. Think about it, this appears to be a rather large basement so, even if one of us finds a way out we'll play hell finding each other again."

"We could call each other," Gray suggested as he held up his cell phone.

"Of course," Kickz agreed. "We just have to exchange numbers."

Each of them prepared to save the others' numbers in their phones when they noticed they had no service.

"Damn," Gray said in frustration. "Must be

because we're in the basement."

Star groaned. "It's a sign I was right in the first place, we're better off staying together! Anyway, think about it, there are a lot of people in this building, and if we found our way down here others probably will too, maybe even some of those freaks. If they find us, we have a better chance together. Ya know, strength in numbers and all that."

Gray nodded in agreement. "Good point. So, we start searching together, and if nothing else, maybe we'll find a landline we can use to call 911."

"Now that we're all on the same page, let's get to it," Kickz said.

The trio searched the various halls and rooms of the basement. They found several conference rooms, supply closets, and mechanical rooms but no exit or phone. Just as Kickz reached for the knob of yet another door they heard footsteps coming from the other end of the hall.

"Could be help," Kickz whispered.

"Could be freaks," Gray countered.

Star held his finger to his lips and motioned for them to go on through the door. They found themselves in a small janitor's closet. Star very softly closed the door. Kickz glanced around and saw a mop leaning against the wall. He quietly put his chair down, retrieved the mop, removed the mop head, and confiscated the thick, wooden handle. They were more on edge than they'd already been as they listened to the footsteps growing ever closer, having no idea who or what was approaching. Each man gripped his makeshift weapon tightly. The footsteps stopped right outside the closet door, and to their horror, the doorknob began to turn. The door opened, and they immediately charged out with their weapons held high. A man stumbled back, nearly losing his footing in the process.

"Shit," the man cried out.

Gray backed off. "Well, he spoke, no growls. Don't think he's going to bite us."

"Course not, bro," the man exclaimed. "I'm not one of those things!"

Star and Kickz lowered their weapons.

"Sorry," Kickz apologized. "We meant no harm. I suppose we're just a little jumpy. I'm Kickz, and this is Star and Gray."

"I've seen your stuff and Star's. Haven't heard of Gray before though. What brings you here," the man asked Gray. "Streamer?"

"Creator," Gray answered. "Just got started a few weeks ago so, I haven't built much of an audience yet, but I've been playing games most of my life. I know who you are though, Kage."

Kage smiled. "My birth certificate says Jim Kage, but in gaming I'm Kage848."

Another man emerged from the room across the hall. Kickz, Star, and Gray instinctively raised their weapons.

"Whoa, whoa, whoa," Kage exclaimed, placing himself in front of the man. "He's cool, guys! He's with me." The men breathed a sigh of relief and lowered their weapons. Kage turned to his friend. "This is Kickz, Star, and Gray."

"I've seen all you guys. I'm Andy Raines or Capp00."

Kickz extended his hand. "I've seen your videos. Nice to meet you."

Star laughed. "No offense, guys, but this is a little messed up. Don't get me wrong, it's absolutely great to have met all of you, but we're standing around talking and shaking hands like we're at some sort of freaking cocktail party while there are freaks upstairs eating people."

"He makes a good point," Capp agreed. "We need a way out. Did any of you find a way out?"

"Unfortunately, no," Kickz answered.

Capp nodded to the room he'd just come from. "I didn't find a way out, but I found something that may come in handy."

Gray smiled when he read the sign next to the door. "You may have found a way out after all."

The others were confused as he walked past them and disappeared into the room.

"What are you both talking about," Kage asked.

"I don't know what he's talking about, but I was referring to the weapons and walkies I found in that security room," Capp replied.

"Exactly," Gray shouted from the room.

The men went to see for themselves what he was talking about. In the security room they found Gray staring at a map on the wall next to several monitors.

"What's this," Star asked.

"I worked as a security guard for a short time, and I learned most security stations in large buildings have a map of the property." Gray pointed to the map. "This should show us where all the entrances and exits are."

"Hell yeah," Kage exclaimed.

"Let's grab walkies and weapons and blow this pop stand," Capp excitedly ordered.

Kickz found the key to the gun cabinet in a desk drawer. Capp passed out radios to each man. Gray studied the map for a moment before taking it down to roll up. Kage and Star searched desks and cabinets for anything that might be useful, such as flashlights and ammo.

"Only four guns," Kickz informed them while handing Star a shotgun and pistols to the others.

Star smiled at the shotgun as if it were an old friend. "Very nice."

Kage looked at the pistol in his hand with disgust. "Seriously?"

"What's wrong, Kage," Capp asked.

Kage held up the weapon. "A pistol, bro! Pistols are crap!" He looked at Star's shotgun longingly.

"Don't even think about it," Star warned.

Gray noticed Kickz didn't have a gun. "What about you Kickz? We need to find another gun for you."

Kickz held up a bat he'd found in a corner of the room. "Nah. I was always more of a melee man myself."

Star's mood shifted. He no longer smiled as he gazed at the shotgun in his hands, and his face was flush with concern. "We all play games, and in those games we use every weapon imaginable, but this isn't a game. Are we maybe overreacting? Have any of us even fired a gun in real life?"

Gray was the first to answer. "Southern boy here. Fired several."

Kickz shook his head. "Never."

"Bounty hunter in real life," Kage declared. "I've had weapons training."

Capp simply replied, "I can shoot."

Kickz pointed to the monitors. "Does that look like we're overreacting?"

The monitors revealed the true carnage taking place on the floors above them. Terrified people were hiding in stairwells, under tables, behind desks, and anywhere they thought they might have a slim chance of survival. Others tried to fend off the crazed freaks with improvised weapons whereas many had obviously given up the fight or been unable to find a safe hiding place and were being devoured. In the corner of one room, an older gentleman huddled with a group of teenagers. They were praying as several deranged cannibals surrounded them. It was painfully apparent what their fate would be.

"Those of us who have experience with guns need to give Kickz and Star a cursory lesson. After that, once we're on our way, we flank their front and rear," Gray suggested.

They spent a short time giving Kickz and Star a crash course in both the pistol and the shotgun. Kickz wondered why he needed it since he wasn't carrying a gun. Capp explained if something happened to one of them, he could increase his chance of survival with the bat and the fallen man's gun. Kickz hated the thought but couldn't deny the truth in what Capp's logic.

Gray led the way through the maze of basement hallways using the map from the security office for guidance. According to the map there were two exits out of the building from the basement itself and another through the parking garage just off the basement. They picked the basement exit that was closest to the security office to make their escape.

"Just up here," Gray told them in a low tone.

Approaching the intersection of two hallways, they could hear what sounded like a faint shuffling of feet. Gray peeked around the corner. He could see the exit at the end of the hall, but he could also see a pack of roughly ten to fifteen cannibals meandering around and making a meal of two security guards. He pulled his head back and quickly informed the others of what he saw.

"Okay, so we go for the other exit, ja," Kickz whispered.

They turned back the direction from which they'd come. They made it to the other basement exit without any issues and were relieved to see there were no obstacles between them and the door to the outside world. Kage pushed the bar to open the door, but it didn't budge. He pushed again and again, increasing his force each time. Still, the door did not open. Capp tried, and he too pushed and pushed, but the door remained closed.

Kage punched the door in frustration. "Damn thing is locked!"

Capp calmly took control of the situation. "It is what it is. We just have to switch gears. Gray, where is the other exit?"

"Through the employee parking garage. It isn't far from here."

"Maybe we should stay down here," Kage suggested. "We could hole up in one of these rooms until help comes."

Star was pleased with the idea. "Yeah, after all, we don't know what is between here and that parking garage. Surely the cops have gotten here by now.

They'll start searching the building any minute now. They'll find us."

"You're right, they are probably here," Capp agreed, "but you saw how many of those things are up there. It will take the police forever to get things under control enough to search the building. What will find us in the meantime?"

They'd all been all too happy to go along with Kage's idea. It was comforting to think of simply sitting back and waiting for the calvary to arrive. It was certainly a much more pleasant thought than possibly running into crazed cannibals in the halls or the parking garage, but they all knew Capp was right. With heavy hearts they decided their best option was indeed to get to the parking garage. Once again, Gray led the way, and in a short time, they arrived at the door to the parking garage.

They entered with caution, being sure to visually scan everything they could see. The group made their way through the garage as quickly and quietly as possible, occasionally stopping behind a car to survey the way ahead. During one such stop they could see the silhouette of someone moving several feet ahead of them. As they watched the figure move, waiting for it to step into the light as to get a better look at it, a middle-aged couple rushed up from behind them.

The woman's eyes were wide, filled with terror. "Can you help us?"

"You're lucky one of us didn't kill you," Capp hissed in a whisper. "Where the hell did you come from?"

"We were hiding under a car back there," the man answered. "When we saw you go by and saw you had weapons, we knew you were normal. Can you help us?"

"Stay down, be quiet, and do as we tell you," Capp firmly ordered.

Not far from the first figure they saw, they could see other figures moving about in the shadows. Gray squinted and strained his eyes in an attempt to count exactly how many there were. As he did the lights began to flicker.

Kickz looked at the flickering light above them. "Oh, this sucks ballz."

"You mean donkey balls," Kage corrected. "Big ole, hairy donkey balls."

The lights flickered a few times more before completely going out and plummeting them into pitch black darkness.

"What's happening," the woman asked in a panic, her voice steadily rising.

"Keep it down," Star ordered.

Kickz reminded them of the flashlights they had, but Kage pointed out the flashlights might attract unwelcome attention.

"Our luck may have run out," Gray stated solemnly.

"Nonsense," Star scolded in a hushed tone. "It ain't over 'til it's over. I'll be damned if I die in a dark, dirty garage. We stay together, tight, and low, and make our way along the wall. Be fast but quiet, and we do not stop for any reason."

"I'm in," Capp proclaimed. "I'm not dying today."

Gray took one last look at the map. "There should be an exit ramp straight ahead."

The group made their way along the wall in tight formation as Star had instructed. The closer they got the more sunlight they could see streaming down the ramp. That sunlight was quite literally a ray of hope however, it also gave them a better glimpse of what awaited them. There were at least a dozen cannibals lumbering at the bottom of the ramp. The sight forced them to stop behind another car close to the ramp.

"What do we do," the man asked.

"Perhaps we should go back," Kickz speculated.

"Go back to what," Kage asked. "A building full of those things? I know I was the one who wanted to hole up, but I was wrong. We need to get out of this building."

Gray agreed. "Our only hope is straight up that

ramp. If we're silent and fast, we can probably get over there with no problems. Then we just have to outrun whoever or whatever is there up the ramp." He took a step forward, accidentally kicking a can in the dark.

The noise drew the attention of the cannibals. They jerked their heads toward the noise, some of their necks making loud cracking sounds. Gray and the others instinctively crouched lower, each one desperately hoping the shadows had kept them hidden.

The woman started to panic again. "Oh, God! Oh, God! They're going to see us! They know we're here," she uttered, her voice again rising.

"Be quiet," Star warned.

She peered at the cannibals, all the while feeling her heart race and fighting the urge to scream. Suddenly she caught a clear glimpse of the back of a rather large police officer standing near the bottom of the ramp. "Thank, God," she exclaimed as she popped straight up from her hiding spot.

"Get the hell down," Capp snapped.

Star turned to her husband. "Shut her up!"

Her husband frantically yanked on her arm. "Honey, be quiet," he pled. "Get back down now!"

"But we're saved! Don't you see him?" She pointed to the officer. "Officer! Sir!" She waved her free arm in the air to get his attention.

The men tried to silence her and pulled at her, but

she persisted. Her movements and shouting agitated the cannibals who snarled, growled, and bit at the air as they started to move toward the group.

"She's going to get us killed," Kage barked at her husband.

Her distraught husband stood up behind her, wrapped one arm around both her waist and arms, and placed his free hand firmly over her mouth. She struggled against him until the officer turned to look at her. Her eyes grew wide with horror. His face was grossly distorted. The shirt of his uniform was open, exposing a horridly swollen abdomen and a bulging wound on his chest. He snarled at her, and it was only then that she realized the cannibals were closing in around them. She broke free of her husband's grip and ran blindly back into the darkness. Her husband instantly dashed after her.

"We have to go get them," Gray told the others.

Capp nodded to the cannibals who were practically on top of them. "I think we're about to have our hands full right here. Time to fight or die, boys!"

Capp jumped up from his crouched position, took aim with his pistol, and fired a round into the stomach of a female cannibal. She grunted and stumbled but regained her footing and continued to advance toward them. He took aim again, his second shot catching her in the forehead. She went down and did not get back up. The other men stood, readied their weapons, and joined him in the fight.

Star's first shot with his newly acquired shotgun completely missed its mark but did pepper cannibals and cars close by. The kick of the weapon surprised him, but he shook it off. He collected himself and took aim at a man with blood running from his ears, eyes, and mouth. His shot hit the man square in the face, dropping him like a ragdoll. Star's lips curled into a satisfied grin. "Yes, baby! Shotgun rain!"

Kickz swung his bat, catching a cannibal's leg and dropping him to one knee. His next swing caught him in the ribs, and a third swing solidly connected with his temple. A sickening crack echoed through the parking garage as the side of the man's skull caved in.

Gray and Kage were consistently hitting their marks, firing round after round, but most of their assailants kept coming. Gray noticed those hit in the head went down and stayed down. With that in mind he decided to perform a fast experiment. He first took careful aim at a cannibal's chest and pulled the trigger, his bullet finding the cannibal's heart. It should have been an instant kill shot, but the cannibal simply stumbled then continued to move forward. Gray then took aim at its head. His aim was true, and the bullet pierced its forehead, and it fell to the floor in a heap.

"Aim strictly for their heads," Gray yelled. "Forget anywhere else, go straight for the head!"

The men did as he said, fighting their way to the bottom of the ramp near the parking attendant's booth where they found the large, deformed officer was waiting for them.

"Really big boy," Kage uttered between heavy breaths as the grotesque man twitched and growled.

"He seems slow," Kickz observed. "I think we can get by him."

Suddenly the officer started to belch and retch.

Star grimaced. "Dude's gonna hurl."

"Yep, and I'm not down to see that. This is our chance, let's go," Capp exclaimed.

The group made a mad dash up the ramp and into the daylight outside. Behind them they heard more retching followed by a loud splatter.

Kage winced. "That sounded nasty."

They squinted and allowed their eyes to adjust to the bright light. It was then they realized the world outside the convention had changed. Sirens blared, and people ran screaming through the streets. A sense of Armageddon loomed in the air. Crazed cannibals wandered among the terrified people, some ripping flesh from victims who'd been unlucky enough to run slower than their friends.

"What the actual hell," Gray muttered to

himself, his companions, and to God.

Out of the blue Kickz stepped toward Capp with his bat raised high. In shock, Capp ducked just as Kickz brought the bat down to land a powerful blow to the top of a cannibal's head behind Capp.

Capp stared at the body lying on the asphalt. "I think I might have soiled myself, but thanks, Kickz."

Approaching on their right was a teenage girl in a dress. It was obvious both she and her dress had been quite pretty at one point but were no longer. Her torn, bottom lip fully exposed her teeth and gums. The front of her dress was covered in blood and bits of flesh, and she made strange, high-pitched sounds. The men gazed upon her with feelings of sadness and loss. Not only was she too young to have her life cut so short, but she was the physical embodiment of the fact all beauty and normalcy in the world had been forever shattered.

The sound of snarling drew their attention back to the parking garage where more cannibals were navigating their way up the ramp. The men glanced around, unsure of what to do or where to go. Near the street corner Star spied a police cruiser with its lights on and driver's door open. When he pointed to it there were no words needed, they all understood. Once again, they found themselves running for their lives. They dodged cannibals who grabbed at them and jumped over bodies until they reached the cruiser. Kickz, Star, and Gray swiftly slid into the backseat, Kage took the passenger's seat up front, and Capp climbed behind the steering wheel. Luck was on their side as the keys were still in the ignition.

As they sped away, Kage noticed a sawed-off shotgun leaning against his seat. "Bye-bye, pistol."

CHAPTER 2

A drive through the streets of Roma made it clear whatever had happened at the convention had also affected the entire city. It looked like a full-blown warzone. Fires burned through buildings and homes, the police and the military fought to hold back droves of cannibals, small explosions erupted, and helicopters circled in the sky. Death and madness were everywhere. The five men in the confiscated police cruiser watched it all in silence, each trying to wrap his mind around what he was seeing. Capp steered the cruiser toward the closest route out of the city only to discover he wasn't the only one who'd had that idea. The road was clogged with hundreds of cars bringing traffic to a standstill.

Kage broke the silence. "Gray, why did you tell us to aim for their heads back there?"

"Just noticed they didn't stay down if they weren't hit in the head. Guess it kind of confirms that part of zed lore."

His response stunned the others.

"Wait a minute," Star said. "Are you saying you think those freaks are zombies? Like walking dead?"

Gray looked at him with a perfectly straight face. "Yes, I am."

"Zombies are a work of fiction," Kage retorted. "Those things back there were very real."

"I wouldn't dismiss the idea so hastily," Kickz cautioned. "All fiction has at least a small basis in reality, and there have been stories of zombies in some form or another in most cultures throughout time."

"And let's not forget there have been many reports of various governments experimenting with reanimating dead tissue for decades," Gray added. "Besides, would you rather believe we just killed a bunch of living people or zombies?"

None of them answered the question, but all of them knew they didn't want to believe they'd killed actual people. For several minutes they discussed theories about what might have caused the outbreak. Kickz remembered the headlines from the newspaper and realized it was still in his back pocket. He showed the paper to the others, speculating the potential conflict and the mysterious illness were related and might be possible causes of the events of the day. Everyone agreed it was a possibility in light of the various biological weapons potentially available.

While waiting for traffic to move they checked their cell phones for a signal. Upon seeing none of them had one Kage started to flip through channels on the cruiser's CB radio. After finding nothing but static, he was about to give up when an announcement came over a channel.

"This is Officer Lindon Mitchell of the Roma Police Department. I am hoping this reaches anyone and everyone with a device capable of receiving the transmission. The city is no longer safe. If you can hear me, evacuate immediately. If you cannot evacuate, find shelter, and secure all doors and windows. Avoid any highly populated areas and stay off the streets. All emergency services are down, and most of the RPD is dead or missing. We are waiting for the military to send additional troops, but we have no idea when or even if that will happen. Again, if you can get out of the city, get out! God help us all."

The men were stunned. None of them spoke a word as the magnitude of what they'd just heard sank in.

The silence was shattered by a frantic, young woman beating on Kage's window. "Please, officers, help!"

Kage rolled the window down. "We're not officers, Miss. The best thing you can do is get back in your car and lock the doors."

"But they've busted the windows," she exclaimed

as she raised a finger to point to a car a few links ahead of them.

The car was under attack by four zombies pounding on its sides. One window had been broken, and the zombies were reaching for the people trapped inside. Just ahead of that car a massive group of zombies were moving between the cars as some people abandoned their vehicles to attempt to escape on foot.

"They're coming this way," Kickz stated nervously.

Kage turned back to the window to tell the young woman to get in, but she was already running away.

Capp looked behind them, and quickly determined the bumper-to-bumper traffic had left him no room to maneuver the cruiser out of it. "We're going to have to make a run for it."

"Run to where," Star asked. "The city is literally burning and has been overrun."

"There is a warehouse not far from here," Gray offered. "I saw it earlier today. Big fence around it with a few vehicles parked inside the fence. If we can get in, maybe we can hide there until things die down a little. Then we can take one of the vehicles and roll out of this city."

Kage sighed. "Anything's better than being here at this moment."

"Okay, we stay close to each other and pay

attention to everything around us. Stay alert, and do not stop for anything," Capp instructed.

Immediately upon stepping out of the cruiser Gray had to execute a zombie that tried to grab him. "Kage, say what you will about pistols, but right now, I am in love with this thing."

Kage smirked. "Well, you and Juliet lead the way, Romeo."

The men methodically made their way in the direction of the warehouse. They passed many people who were running in a blind panic, and Gray wondered what was preventing the five of them from reacting in the same manner. Was it something in their pasts? Maybe something in their present lives? Perhaps, their gaming backgrounds had mentally prepared them for such an event? Gray didn't know why those questions were important to him at that moment, but he did know he wished they were simply playing a game.

Hiding behind a dumpster, they visually scouted out the warehouse across the alley from the dumpster. They were relieved that area of the city was mostly clear of people and zombies. Screams from the main street could still be heard, but it appeared no one had tried to escape through that route or hide in that area. The eight-foot-tall fence around the warehouse had a gate secured with a heavy chain and lock, signaling to them they would have to climb over. At that point they would have been willing to climb Mount Everest to reach some sort of safety. Needless to say, the fence did nothing to deter them. Cautiously, they left their hiding place. Just as they reached the alley a bloody woman ran to them from the main street.

"They're coming! Please, help me," she screamed before collapsing at their feet.

Capp was helping her up when a large group of zombies rounded the corner from the street. Kickz hurriedly assisted Capp in getting the woman up. Each of them put one of her arms over their shoulders to support her, and that's when Kickz noticed the bite marks on her arms. Her head hung so low her face wasn't quite visible, and she was babbling incoherently. Ahead of them, Gray and Kage had made it over the fence. Star was about to start his climb when he decided to turn back to help Capp and Kickz.

"Don't you dare," Capp shouted. "Get over that fence!"

Strange sounds came from the badly injured woman. Although Kickz recognized the sounds right away as being very similar to the ones Lou made, it was too late. She jerked her head up in that now all too familiar, unnatural way and lunged for Kickz's throat. He freed himself from under her arm only to fall backward. Capp grabbed the woman by the shoulders. Despite being a strong man and outweighing her by a good eighty pounds, he struggled to pull her off. She was not a large woman, she was actually quite small, yet she possessed the strength of ten men. As Capp tried to wrestle her off Kickz a large, male zombie grabbed the back of Capp's neck with its meaty hands and pushed him to the ground. Capp attempted to roll away, but he couldn't escape the massive creature.

Star was halfway up the warehouse fence when he heard the commotion. Without hesitation he jumped down and ran to their aid. Realizing he didn't have a weapon because he'd already thrown his shotgun over the fence to Kage, his eyes darted around the alley in search of anything he could use against the monsters attacking his companions. He saw a thick board near the dumpster, retrieved it, and proceeded to whack the woman on the back of the head with all the force he could muster. It took three strikes before she dropped and rolled off to the side of Kickz.

Star helped Kickz to his feet. "You okay?"

"Ja. Ja, I'm fine."

The horde of zombies from the street was closing in. Kickz and Star turned their attention to Capp who'd managed to stand up and was fending off the large zombie along with another they hadn't noticed before in the chaos. Gray and Kage opened fire on the horde through the fence, but they were only able to pick off a few before the horde reached the others at the same time more zombies began to emerge from between buildings in the alley.

"Go," Capp screamed at Kickz and Star. "Go now! Don't stop for anything, remember? Move your asses!"

The last thing Kickz or Star wanted was to leave Capp, but a fast evaluation of the situation told them they had very little choice. Kage and Gray continued to fire on the horde as Star and Kickz ran to the fence. Upon reaching it, Kickz threw his bat over before they started to climb. Star had made it only about a foot up when he felt a sharp yank on his leg. He looked down to see a zombie had hold of his ankle and others were reaching for him. Gray stuck the barrel of his pistol through the fence and discharged a bullet directly through the eye of the zombie gripping Star's ankle. Once free, Star rapidly scaled the fence. Kickz, Kage, Gray, and Star searched for any glimpse of Capp, but the horde had swarmed the fence, preventing them from seeing anything other than the undead mass.

Reluctantly accepting there was little hope Capp had survived, the remaining men looked for a way into the warehouse. Kage found a crowbar and a pipe in the back of a pickup parked in front of the warehouse. He used them to pry up a loading dock door enough for them to slide under. Once inside they did a sweep of the building but found it to be empty. After closing the loading dock door, they hunkered down in an upstairs office. The utterly exhausted men collapsed onto chairs and the floor.

Kickz looked at each man directly before saying what they'd all accepted but didn't want to vocalize. "There's no way Capp survived. I'd known the man only a few hours yet, he died trying to save me. I don't even know if he had family or anything about him really. Did any of you?"

Star and Gray shook their heads somberly.

"I did," Kage admitted. "I met him a few years ago at another con. Since then we've talked a lot and met up several times. He was a good guy, and he did have a family at one point. He was a veteran too, did two tours in the desert."

"What happened to his family," Gray inquired.

Kage sighed heavily. "He had a wife and a daughter. About a year ago his wife was killed in a car wreck. She was seven months pregnant with a baby boy. Between losing his wife and son and what he experienced in the military, he just lost it. He withdrew from everybody and everything, including his little girl. His daughter ended up living with his wife's parents. He only recently got back into gaming and making videos. Not sure what it was, but something was snapping him out of it. He was even planning on bringing his daughter home after this convention."

A growl interrupted the conversation.

The sound put Kage on high alert. "What the hell was that?"

"My stomach," Star sheepishly answered.

The others broke into laughter, and in spite of himself, Star laughed too.

"Jesus, Star! Sounded like a bear," Gray teased through his laughter.

"Hey, I'm a twenty-year-old college student, a growing boy!"

Star's reply only served to evoke more laughter.

"Question is, what the hell are you growing into," Kickz roared.

Even though they found the volume of Star's rumbling stomach comical it reminded them they could all do with a bite to eat. After searching through the office, they moved to the breakroom where they found a drink machine but not much else. Kage again put the crowbar to work, using it to pry the machine open, enabling them to at least have a drink. The breakroom had a large window overlooking the main storage area of the warehouse. Gray casually looked out the window to the boxes stacked below as he sipped his soda. After a few more sips, his curiosity overcame him, and he made his way down the stairs to the storage area while Kage, Kickz, and Star sat at a table talking. Gray used his pocketknife to open one of the first boxes he came to. He grinned like a Cheshire cat when he saw the contents of the box.

"Hey, guys," he shouted. "Come here. Hurry up!"

The others ran down the stairs with their weapons readied.

"What happened," an alarmed Kickz asked.

Gray tossed Star something small wrapped in plastic. "Maybe that'll pacify that bear of yours."

Star looked at the small package in his hands. It was a snack cake with a label that read, "Armageddon Snacks, So Good They'll Slaughter Your Tastebuds."

"You've got to be kidding me," Star groaned. "I'm still gonna eat it, but you've got to be kidding me."

The men took their snack cake booty back to the office to satiate their hunger and were never so grateful for sugary pastries in their lives.

Kickz finished another cake and washed it down with some soda, all the while Capp was on his mind. "What happened to Capp could happen to any of us. We've survived the unthinkable together thus far, don't you think we should get to know one another, if for no other reason than, God forbid, one of us doesn't make it, we can be remembered properly? Everyone deserves that."

Star was the first to tell his story. "I'm twenty, and my real name is David Star. I'm from Chicago, and I'm in college, taking courses in computer science. I love everything about computers, but I love to cook too so, I've been taking culinary classes on the side and working at a restaurant part time. No kids and not married, not even a girlfriend. Between school, work, and making videos I don't have time to form any kind of meaningful relationships. I always wanted to and even thought one day I'd want kids. Maybe, hopefully, when the dust settles, there will be a few girls with a pulse left. If so, might be time for me to slow down and try to form more than a passing acquaintance with somebody."

Kage volunteered to be next. "My real name is Jim Kage, from Washington state, and a bounty hunter by trade. I'm forty-two with no kids, but I was married once. It didn't end very well, and since then, I've made it a point to keep everyone at arm's length. I didn't think anyone could be worth risking going through that hell again." He waved a hand toward Star. "After this, I may have to take a page from the kid's book and truly get to know somebody."

"Guess I'll go next," Gray offered. "I'm forty and from Emporia, Virginia. Currently I'm a maintenance supervisor at a computer component manufacturing plant. Not a bad job, pay is good, but sometimes it really gets under my skin. There's a bunch of people there who think because they were trained to solder a diode to a board, they're suddenly computer experts. Anyway, no wife or kids, but I do sort of have a girlfriend. It's complicated. I love gaming, but music is my first love, I play drums. Oh, and my real name is Pete Lewis."

Kickz took a deep breath. "Well, the real name is Jason Fran, and I am also forty. I was born and raised in Germany but moved to Ireland several years ago, thus the confusing accent. I am married with one child, a son. I own a pc building and repair business, and I am a programmer as well. I love my work and my family. I'm hoping they're okay. Currently I am sitting in the middle of the apocalypse with three men I now consider friends."

Kage raised his soda. "Here's to surviving the apocalypse with friends."

The group of men talked late into the night about a variety of topics. Periodically, one of them made a sweep of the building to ensure it was still secure and check the status of the horde. The horde had thinned out, but many zombies remained lined up along the fence. The group thought the remaining zombies would be gone by morning. It was decided they would leave in one of the vehicles in the parking lot the following morning. Until then, being sore and exhausted, they would keep watch and sleep in shifts. Kage took the first watch.

Sitting in a chair against the office door with his shotgun across his lap, he could barely hear the hungry mob moaning at the fence. The clock on the wall seemed to be louder than they were, and Kage found its rhythmic ticking to be very soothing. It was approaching an hour into his shift when that ticking and his exhaustion started to get the better of him. He fought the urge to doze off as long as he could but ultimately drifted off to sleep. He'd only been asleep for a few minutes when a noise outside the office door woke him. Seeing that the others didn't stir, he thought he'd dreamed it, but then he heard it again. He gripped his shotgun and strained to hear anything else. The soothing tick of the clock became a loud annoyance. The doorknob jiggled next to his head. In one swift movement he was on his feet, facing the door with his shotgun raised. Thankfully, they'd been able to lock the door from the inside, but Kage knew the cheap lock would merely slow down whatever was on the other side of the door, not completely stop it.

Gray woke up, and upon seeing Kage's stance, woke Kickz and Star. The three of them quietly gathered their weapons and stood behind Kage. Gray motioned to Kage to open the door.

Kage gently removed the chair before

unlocking the door. “On three,” he whispered. “One, two, three!”

He threw open the door, and they froze in shock when they saw what was standing on the other side.

Capp smirked. “What is wrong with you people,” he asked sarcastically as he stepped into the room. “You’re always trying to kill me! Please, put the guns away.” He noticed the snack cakes. “Did you at least save me something to eat?”

“How are you here,” Kickz asked in awe.

Capp picked through the snacks until he found one to suit his taste. “No zombies along the fence so, it was fairly easy to get over it. From there, I found an unlocked window and climbed through. No big deal.”

“Bro,” Kage started, “that’s what you’ve got to say? We thought you were dead!”

Capp casually took a bite of his snack. “Guess it’s a good thing you didn’t bet any money on it then. Or did you?”

Gray was stunned. “Man, I’m thrilled to see you. You seriously have no idea how thrilled I think we all are, but how the hell did you survive?”

“Oh, that? I dealt with worse in the military. Now, what’s the plan?”

The others wanted more explanation, but Capp’s demeanor told them he was done with that part of the conversation.

CHAPTER 3

The next morning the group was pleased to find nearly all the horde had moved on apart from a few stragglers. That combined with finding the keys to a box truck tucked away in its sun visor made them feel as if the heavens were smiling upon them. After some discussion, they decided to load several boxes of Armageddon Snacks onto the truck along with anything possessing the potential to be used as a weapon.

"We need to get out of Roma," Kickz stated. "Maybe outside the city or outside the county hasn't been affected as badly, perhaps not at all. So, we should find somewhere to get plenty of fuel."

Kage wedged the crowbar into the chain holding the gate closed and twisted. After a minute of putting considerable tension on it, the chain snapped. Kage manned the gate while the others climbed into the truck. Kickz was driving, Capp was in the passenger's seat, and Star and Gray were in the cargo area.

Kickz pulled the truck up to the gate, and Kage slid it open. A few stragglers left over from the horde wandered through the open gate. Star and Gray got out of the truck to help Kage dispose of them, Kage with his trusty crowbar, and Star and Gray with pipes they'd found in the warehouse. Once the trio was safely in the cargo area of the truck, Kickz eased it into the alley, running over bodies of zombies, including the woman who'd attacked him the day before. Maneuvering the truck through the city streets was no easy task as vehicles, debris, and bodies littered them, but Kickz managed without any major complications arising.

"You handle this thing pretty well," Capp complimented.

"I drove a furniture delivery truck to work my way through college. My bosses expected me to perform miracles with that thing, always expecting me to squeeze it into places it was never meant to go."

Capp chuckled. "If I could meet them now, I'd thank them."

"Ja, I never knew they were preparing me for the apocalypse."

"Reminds me of some of the guys I served with. They could move anything through that desert. Around mines, barricades, you name it, they could do it," Capp recalled with admiration, fondness, and sadness.

The trio in the back of the truck left the door rolled up, partially to avoid suffocating in the heat and partially to allow them to see and deal with any dangers approaching from the rear. From the open door they observed the massive devastation that had fallen on the city. It was worse than it had been the previous day with one very notable difference, there were no longer any screams. Each time the truck's wheels rolled over another body the sound echoed in the back of the truck. The fact the day before those bodies had been living, breathing human beings with lives, friends, and families was not lost on any of them.

Apart from a few abandoned emergency and military vehicles, the lane heading into the city was clear. In contrast, the lane leaving the city was clogged with bumper-to-bumper abandoned vehicles.

Kickz observed the traffic jam before them. "That's one miracle I can't make happen." He pointed to the other lane. "What do you think? Should we?"

Capp grinned. "I don't think you have to worry about getting a ticket."

Kickz agreed and proceeded to start easing the truck across the median when Gray jumped from the back of the truck and ran up to the driver's side window.

Gray pointed to the emergency and military vehicles. "We should check those. They may have things we can use, especially weapons, ammo, or medical supplies."

Capp squirmed in his seat. He wanted no part of going near the military vehicles, but he couldn't deny the solid logic in Gray's thinking.

The men fanned out to search the vehicles but made sure to stay within eyesight of each other. Capp searched an ambulance with no luck. Apparently, someone else had already looted it. The next vehicle he came to was a military truck. He could feel his heart racing as he approached it and swallowed hard to try to rid his throat of the lump he felt in it. Determined to help the group, he marched forward and yanked open the passenger's side door. Instantly he stumbled a few paces back, startled by a soldier in full fatigues sitting in the driver's seat. A gunshot wound on his temple made it obvious the man was no longer living or undead, but the sight of him shook Capp to the core. Images of his time at war flashed through his mind. Raw, unpleasant emotions flowed through him just as surely as his own blood did. His heart raced faster, his ears rang, and he started to sweat profusely.

Gray was searching another military truck

close by and happened to look Capp's direction. He could see he didn't look quite right and thought it prudent to check on him. Drawing closer to Capp, he could see the dead soldier. Having known many veterans in his life, it was easy for Gray to put two and two together. Before Capp noticed him, he turned on his heels and ran back to the truck he'd been searching.

"Hey, Capp," he called as he leaned against the side of the truck. "Capp, I need a hand! Something's wrong. Man, please!"

The sound of Gray's distressed voice pulled Capp out of his awful memories. Fearing Gray was injured he rushed to him. "What's wrong? What happened?"

Gray shook his head. "I don't know. I got dizzy all of a sudden. Maybe it's the heat. Can you help me back to the box truck?"

"Could be the heat, having nothing but sugar to eat, dehydration, or anything. I got you though."

Back at the box truck, Capp retrieved a bottled water for Gray. Gray thanked him and made a point of taking a large drink. Kickz and the others returned shortly, having had about the same luck as Capp and Gray.

"Somebody has to have been through here and looted everything already," Kage speculated.

"And the journey continues," Star sighed.

Once back on the road, they traveled another ten miles before coming across a small gas station. The pumps were blocked by several cars, and the parking lot was full, but there were no signs of life anywhere. Kickz parked the truck on the road in front of the station, and the men cleared the parking lot of the few zombies loitering around. Afterwards, Kage, Capp, and Star searched the cars at the pumps for anything useful and moved them away from the pumps while Kickz and Gray went into the building.

Upon entering the store, the first thing that struck them was how music still playing over the speakers increased the creep factor of the stillness in the empty store. Gray turned the gas pumps on, and the duo set about sweeping each aisle and the restrooms to be certain they had no unwanted guests. Feeling confident they were alone, they grabbed bags from behind the register to fill with supplies. A rack beside a wine cooler display grabbed Gray's attention. It held various medicines for cough, cold, and pain. As much as he hated to admit it, it had been years since he'd exerted himself as much physically as he'd done since things fell apart at the convention, and he could feel it in every part of his body. Deciding to take all the medicine on the rack, he wondered if the rest of the group was feeling the same.

Kickz, holding bags full of an array of goods,

joined him by the rack. "I'm going to run these out to the truck and be right back."

Kickz turned to head for the door when a thumping sound from behind the wine cooler display stopped him in his tracks. Both men dropped their bags and pulled their weapons, ready to defend themselves against whatever fresh hell was coming for them. They saw a door mostly hidden behind the display. They rolled the display out of the way and braced themselves before Gray flung the door open. Before them sat a small, brown chihuahua. The little dog growled and backed away from them. Gray peered into the room which amounted to little more than a storage closet. A small pet carrier with food and water dishes sat in a corner.

"Perhaps the dog belonged to the proprietor," Kickz proposed.

"That or an employee." Gray bent to pick up the still growling dog. "It's okay, little one." Despite Gray's gentle handling and soothing reassurances, the frightened animal promptly bit his hand. However, Gray kept his voice steady and stroked the dog's back.

Kickz was amused. "Tiny thing thinks it's a pit bull."

"Yeah, but we can't leave him. Wait, are you a him?" He peeked to determine the gender of the pooch. "Yep, you're a him."

"I suppose you're right. No living creature should

be left alone in this hell."

Kickz took his bags to the truck then returned to help Gray collect his bags and the dog's things. On their way out they stopped by an aisle with pet supplies to retrieve dog food, treats, and a leash. The rest of the men had just finished clearing a path to the pumps when Kickz and Gray emerged from the store with their new friend.

"What is that," Star asked.

"What's it look like," Gray retorted.

Kage reached out to pet the dog. "Hey there, little fella." The animal greeted him with a growl and show of teeth. "Wow! He's got my ex-wife's attitude."

A mischievous grin played on Capp's lips. "At least we know he has standards," he ribbed.

"Hardy-har-har," Kage grumbled.

Star held up a rifle and a pistol. "What we found isn't nearly as cute as what you found, but they can also exhibit a bad attitude if required."

Kickz nodded his approval. "At this stage of the game we can't have too many weapons. Better to be op than nerfed."

Kickz pulled the truck to the pumps to fill the tank, and the dog was placed safely into its carrier and put in the back of the truck. While the tank was filling, the group conversed about what their next step should be, settling on going to Phoenix. The theory was the capital city of the state would have surely been secured and protected. The drive would take an estimated twenty hours, so the group settled in for a long and uncertain ride.

In the back of the truck Star watched Gray remove the dog from its carrier and handfeed it treats. "Gray, what are you going to call him?"

"I honestly haven't thought about it."

"You could name him after my ex, it would fit," Kage jested.

Star was suddenly struck by a strong smell that caused him to hold his nose. "What is that stench?"

Kage smelled it too. "Whatever it is, it's putrid. Maybe something stuck in the tires? We did run over a few bodies."

They heard a faint noise which was followed by an increase in the stench. At that point they realized it was emanating from somewhere around Gray.

"Dude, that's nasty," Star yelled.

"It wasn't me," Gray swore.

They heard the noise again but realized it was actually the dog passing gas.

Kage covered his nose. "Dang dog! How does something like that come out of something so small?"

A devilish grin spread across Gray's face. "I don't know, but I think I'll name him Tooter."

CHAPTER 4

Kickz had been driving nearly six hour, and the sun was starting to set when he spied something on the road ahead of them. Drawing nearer, he could see it was a van with the hood raised. A handful of people were standing around it.

Capp, who had dozed off, stirred in the passenger's seat. "What's going on?"

"Looks like some people may have broken down."

Capp sat up more in his seat. "Actual breathing type people?"

"It would appear so."

Kickz brought the truck to a stop, and the men got out. They were greeted by a young, blonde woman.

"Thank you so much for stopping. The hunk of junk threw a rod. We're stuck."

"How many of you are there," Capp asked.

"Me, my boyfriend, my two brothers, and a teenage girl we picked up a few miles back. It'll be dark soon, and we don't want to be stuck out here."

Gray motioned toward the box truck. "It's no limo, but it runs, and we have room."

Kage interrupted them. "Uh, could you excuse us for one minute," he asked the strangers. "Gray, guys, can we speak back here," he requested, leading them to the back of the box truck. "I don't want to be an ass, but are we sure this is a good idea? At the very least, shouldn't we discuss these decisions first?"

"I should have consulted with all of you first," Gray said apologetically. "It was instinct to invite them. We can't leave them here though."

"Of course, we won't leave them," Kickz assured.

Kage shook his head slowly. "Look, I don't want to leave them here either, but what do we know about them? Do they want to take our truck or weapons? Is one of them sick with whatever the hell is turning people into monsters? In my line of work I see people every day who can spin a convincing sob story and appear legit, but in reality, they've done evil shit. I'm just saying, considering the current state of affairs, we have to be careful."

"He's right," Capp admitted. "It sucks, but he's right. I had to face situations like this when I was deployed. Horrible position to be in, but caution is best."

Star had remained silent until that point. "I

can't believe what I'm hearing! Capp, man, I get what you're saying, I really do. Hell, I get what Kage is saying, but you're talking about criminals and war! These are people in the same crappy predicament we are!"

Capp stared at him, a large part of himself wishing he could be more like the young man standing before him, that he wasn't so jaded. "Yep, I was talking about war. Do you not think this is a war? Did you not see what I saw in Roma," he demanded sternly.

Kickz, who always wanted to keep the peace, intervened. "You all have valid arguments; therefore, we need to find a happy medium. We should take them with us, otherwise we are no better than monsters ourselves. However, we're no fools either. We should search them and have them turn over any weapons they may have."

"I can get behind that," Gray declared as he looked to the other men who nodded their amenability.

A bloodcurdling scream broke up their huddle. The young blonde's boyfriend was being pulled to the ground by two zombies, and she was trying to beat them off with a lug wrench while her brothers fended off zombies moving in on them. The teen girl ran wildly up the road, disappearing over a rise.

"Where did they come from," Star asked the young woman after he used his shotgun to put down the zombies tearing into her boyfriend's flesh.

She pointed to the woods. "There!"

"I think we've got a problem," Star called to the others upon seeing dozens of zombies emerging from the shadows of the trees.

A simple yet stressed reply came from Kage. "We know!"

Star turned toward Kage's voice to see more zombies coming from the woods on the opposite side of the road. Suddenly he felt a tug on his pant leg. It was the woman's boyfriend.

"Keep her safe," he begged in a strained, raspy voice. "Get her out of here."

"I will not leave you," the young woman forcefully proclaimed as she knelt next to him.

He reached up to wipe away her tears with a trembling, bloody hand. "I'm not going to make it. We both know that, but you can make it. You have to, you have to do it for both of us."

Star watched the scene unfold before him. He knew there was no hope of the man surviving, he was as good as dead, yet Star didn't feel right leaving him to be devoured by the encroaching zombie mass.

"We gotta go," Capp warned.

The blonde woman was holding her dying boyfriend's hand and sobbing uncontrollably. Star pulled her up and handed her off to her brothers.

"Get her to the truck," Star ordered.

Star's demeanor concerned Kickz. "Star, what are you doing?"

"Just get them all to the truck!"

Kickz knew from the tone of Star's voice it was important he did as he asked. "Let's go," he shouted as he ushered everyone to the truck. "Move it!" He stopped at the front of the truck to look back at Star. "You'll hurry, ja?"

"Right behind you. Go!"

"Promise you'll protect her," the dying man demanded.

Star knelt next to him. "I promise I will, but right now I want to help you. I can leave you a weapon, or I can do it for you, but I won't leave you for those monsters. Your choice."

The mortally injured man understood what he meant. "I always seem to mess things up. Could you, please?"

Star stood, pulled a pistol from his waistband, and aimed at the man's forehead.

The man smiled up at him. "Thank you."

Star pulled the trigger, ending his suffering. "I'm so sorry," he whispered.

Kickz watched the act of mercy from behind the steering wheel of the box truck. He was in awe of the courage and compassion displayed by his young comrade. Capp, sitting next to Kickz, also watched. He felt a sense of pride in Star's courageous action but also felt the same sense of heartbreak he'd experienced every time he'd seen a soldier forced to do something no human should ever have to do, particularly someone so young.

Star sprinted to the truck, the zombies entirely too close for comfort. "Roll this thing out," he shouted to Kickz as he ran by his window.

Climbing into the back of the truck, the first thing Star saw was the still sobbing woman being comforted by her brothers. He knew he'd done the right thing, but he was flooded with overwhelming guilt as he watched her.

Gray hadn't actually seen what had transpired between Star and the unlucky man, but he had seen the man's injuries and heard the shot. He was fairly certain he knew what had happened. Since meeting Star, he'd had the impression he was very laid-back and kept things lighthearted. Gray wondered how that same laid-back, young man had summoned the strength to do something he doubted he could have done himself and what impact it would have on Star.

Kage opened fire on the zombies through the truck's open door. He found it felt good to watch them fall. He hated them. He hated them for the position they'd put Star in, and he hated them for turning the world upside down. With every whimper of the distraught woman he hated them even more.

Kickz steered the truck around the van, past the man's body, and over the rise the teenager had disappeared over only moments before. On the other side of the rise, they discovered her fate. She lay in the middle of the road, clearly dead, and being eaten.

They rode in silence for quite some time. The young woman cried herself to sleep, her head resting on her brother's lap. From where he sat on the opposite side of the truck, Star tried in vain to avoid looking at her. She was beautiful, but he felt physically ill every time he looked at her.

The brother being used as a pillow looked down at her then at Star. "I'm Chris. Thank you for what you did."

The other brother nodded. "Yes, thank you. I'm Jordan."

"Nothing to thank me for," Star somberly replied.

Chris disagreed. "Amber is alive because of you. She never would have left him if you hadn't intervened."

"It's true," Jordan said. "Thanks to you, we still have our sister, and Kevin didn't have to suffer. You did the best thing that could have been done, and it was a favor to both of them."

Star appreciated their words, but they weren't of any comfort.

After hours of traveling, Kickz stopped the truck.

"I've got to pee and stretch," he told Capp.

Capp stretched in his seat. "I could water the weeds myself."

Amber woke up when the truck stopped. "What's happening?"

"Probably a pee break," Kage answered. "Everybody stay put while I check it out though." With that, he cautiously hopped out of the back of the truck.

Tooter started to whimper, and Gray removed him from his carrier. "You have to pee too, buddy," Gray asked the tiny pooch.

"He's cute," Amber commented. "Is he yours?"

"I guess he is now. We found him at a gas station a way back."

"Coast is clear," Kage announced from outside.

Everyone got out to stretch their legs and take a bathroom break if needed. Tooter promptly trotted over to a clump of weeds and hiked his legs.

"That pup has the right idea," Jordan snickered before walking a short distance away to relieve himself.

Amber proceeded toward a small patch of bushes and tall weeds off the side of the road with Star right on her heels. "Where are you going," he inquired.

"I have to pee. Is that okay with you?"

"You shouldn't go off alone."

Amber never broke her stride. "You don't have

to worry. My mama potty trained me a long time ago. I can handle it all by myself."

"It's not safe," Star persisted.

Amber was clearly annoyed. "I don't need a babysitter," she informed him as she walked into the bushes ahead of him.

Star heard the distinct sound of a zipper, and Amber disappeared behind the bush. He was stunned and turned his back to her. "Are you really doing that?"

"Uh-huh. Don't you ever pee?"

"Of...Of course I do," Star stumbled over his words. "I just don't do it in front of people."

"Technically, I'm behind you," she stated smugly. "Anyway, nobody asked you to come along, creeper." She stood, pulling her pants up.

"I made a promise to keep you safe, and I don't break my word."

Amber stepped from the bush and around him so as to face him. "A promise, huh? Cause you're such a noble guy? Funny, I didn't see that noble guy anywhere around when you ripped me away from my boyfriend and executed him." She spat her words like venom.

Star was taken aback, her words cutting him like razors. "Screw you," he managed to whisper.

"Excuse me!"

"You heard me!" His voice grew louder with each word until it roared from him. "Screw you, chick!"

"You're an ass," she growled, turning on her heels to go back to the truck.

Star watched her walk away as his mind raced. Was that really what he'd done? Had he done the right thing, or had he executed Kevin? Literally shaking his head to clear his mind of those thoughts, he went after her, catching up to her as she rejoined the rest of the group. "Yeah, I can be an ass," he shouted. "Anybody who ever knew me can tell you I can be an ass, just like anybody else can be, but I am no murderer! You're grieving and will have to live with his loss the rest of your life, but I'll carry his death and your pain for the rest of mine! Trust me, it won't be a picnic!"

He stormed past them all on his way to the cab of the truck. They heard the passenger's side door open and slam shut.

"I guess that means he called shotgun," Kage joked in an effort to lighten the mood.

Those who were going to ride in the back of the truck settled in with drinks and snacks. Kickz grabbed himself a soda and snack and started for the driver's side of the cab when Capp pulled him aside.

"You've been driving for hours. Why not let me drive for a while," Capp offered. "You have to be exhausted."

Kickz was indeed tired, but he suspected Capp had ulterior motives, and he understood them. “That would be terrific. I could do with a break.”

Capp gathered a couple of drinks and a few snack cakes. Sliding into the driver’s seat he offered a drink and cake to Star. “Bet you’re starving.”

“Not really.”

Capp lightly shook the offering at Star, but when he spoke, his tone was firm. “Maybe not, but all of us have to keep our strength and energy up.”

Star reluctantly took the drink and cake.

In the back of the truck, Amber sat between her brothers, futilely trying to get comfortable on the hard floor. She was squirming when she saw Chris eyeing her. “What?”

“I love you, little sister, but you can be selfish and thick at times.”

Jordan threw his head back and laughed. “It’s officially the end of the world, folks! Me and Chris agree on something!”

“What are you idiots babbling about,” Amber demanded.

Chris motioned to the cab of the truck. “That guy up there not only saved you, he saved Kevin too. He saved him in the only way he could be saved, and you should be grateful.”

CHAPTER 5

Capp had never been the best conversationalist, struggling with simple small talk, so tough or serious conversations were particularly hard for him. There were many things he wanted to say to Star. He desperately wanted to help him process what he knew the young man was surely feeling, but he couldn't find the words to even begin. Thus, they rode in silence, save for the static from the radio Star turned on in hopes of hearing some news. After thirty minutes or so of that, Capp believed he'd figured out how to approach the conversation, but as he opened his mouth to speak, a beeping started.

Capp's heart sank when he looked at the dash. "Not good."

"What's not good," Star questioned. "We've had more than enough not good for today."

"I agree with you, but that was the low fuel warning. If we don't find gas soon, we're going to have more not good."

Star rolled his eyes. “Stranded in the dark. This day just keeps getting better and better.”

Capp was filled with relief when he looked ahead up the road. “Hell, maybe it actually is.”

Star saw it too. “Well, wonders never cease.”

Ahead of them was a Danterford’s Emporium sign, shining in the truck’s headlights like a beacon of hope. Danterford’s Emporium was a big box superstore. At Danterford’s one could purchase groceries, clothing, pet supplies, housewares, and gas among other things. Capp’s relief swiftly turned into concern as he remembered Danterford’s stores were always located in or near decently sized towns, so it stood to reason they were possibly heading into a heavily populated area. Would it be overrun like Roma? Apparently, the same thought crossed Star’s mind because he used the walkie he’d gotten at the convention to radio Gray in the back, making the others aware of the situation.

Kickz pulled the door down as far as he could without latching it and locking them in, but about a twelve inch gap remained. Because the door was spring loaded he was forced to hold it in place. Kage trained the rifle he’d swapped his shotgun for on the door, and the three siblings gripped metal pipes. Gray returned Tooter to his carrier and picked up the shotgun Kage had previously discarded. They felt like fish in a barrel.

Capp steered the truck to the gas pumps, trying to avoid accelerating much in order to keep the truck as quiet as possible. Star held tightly to his shotgun, his eyes darting about the parking lot. It was well lit, but the store itself looked as if it might have been closed when the world fell. He saw no signs of anyone, living or dead, but he knew they couldn't afford to let their guard down. He radioed Gray again, telling him they should stay in the back until he or Capp came to get them. Capp shut the truck off, and they exited the cab.

Capp swiftly unscrewed the truck's gas cap while Star covered him. For a brief moment Capp allowed himself to think the whole ordeal would go smoothly and they'd be back on the road within a matter of minutes. He lifted the nozzle from the pump, flipped the lever, and instantly felt nauseous when nothing happened.

Star saw the look on Capp's face. "What's wrong," he whispered.

"The pumps aren't on."

Gray and Kage slipped around the side of the truck to join them.

"Sorry, we were feeling a little anxious just waiting back there," Gray explained.

"What's the holdup," Kage asked.

Star was clearly frustrated. "Damned pumps are off."

They looked at the small attendant's booth

positioned at the end of the pumps. A light inside the booth flickered. Someone would need to go inside to turn the pumps on. Gray reminded them he'd only had to flip a switch and push a button to turn the pumps on at the last station and volunteered to do it again. Kage informed him it wouldn't be that easy. He explained the other store had been a small, rural store and probably used an older system whereas most stores, especially large chains, used a computerized system.

Kage explained how he'd acquired that knowledge. "My ex's parents owned a chain franchise, I used to help them out."

The four men decided Kage and Gray would go get the pumps on while Capp and Star covered them. The booth only had a few small windows, and they were protected by thick bars, preventing easy entry. Kage and Gray went to the side of the tiny, block building where they found a locked door.

"We don't want to make a lot of noise getting that door open," Gray pointed out. "What do we do?"

"I've got a trick I could try," Kage answered as he pulled his wallet from his back pocket. "Grab the crowbar for me."

Kage pulled a credit card from his wallet, and Gray returned within seconds with the requested crowbar. Kage wedged the crowbar between the door and doorframe a couple of inches above the lock. Applying some torque he was able to bend that section of the door out ever so slightly and with minimal noise. Still applying pressure to the crowbar with one hand, he used the other hand to slide the credit card into the opening and down to the lock. After some maneuvering, he was able to slide the card between the latch and the strike plate and easily open the door.

"Do I want to know where you learned to do that," Gray asked.

Kage gave him a cockeyed grin. "Movies."

They crept quietly into the building. The booth consisted of the main room containing the register and customer service window and a cramped bathroom with a dirty toilet and sink. The compact nature of the building made it easy to do a fast sweep of the building. Seeing no zombies, they determined they were alone.

Kage stepped to the register. "This is strange. It's on and in operation mode. They must have been open when the shit hit the fan, but the door was locked. So, where is the attendant?"

"Maybe they ran for the hills. Blame them? Minimum wage ain't worth dying for."

"True, but why take the time to lock the door if you're running for your life," Kage puzzled.

Kage pushed the question from his mind to focus on the task at hand. He moved his fingers quickly, authorizing the two pumps closest to the truck. As he finished something under the counter grabbed his foot, and he felt pressure on his shoe. Looking down he saw a teenage boy who had obviously been afflicted with whatever was turning people into flesh-eating freaks. The boy had hold of Kage's foot and was attempting to chew through his shoe. Gray pulled Kage back, and the boy crawled out from under the counter. The nametag on his shirt introduced him as Toby. He was about to get to his feet when Gray raised his shotgun, but Kage stopped him.

"The noise," Kage warned. "Besides, it will deafen us in here."

Gray lowered the weapon. "We're so sorry this happened to you, Toby." He raised his foot and firmly planted it in the back of Toby's head.

Kage used the butt of his rifle to repeatedly strike the boy's head until the contents of his skull spilled onto the floor. Once Toby was no longer a threat, they checked Kage's shoe and were ecstatic to see Toby hadn't managed to chew through it.

"Who knows if it even spreads through bites? Messed up situation when the only clue we have to whatever the hell this is and however the hell it spreads is movie lore," Kage stated with disgust.

Gray felt badly about what they'd done to poor Toby, and he agreed with Kage, but he couldn't resist a smart aleck retort. "Well, you did learn breaking and entering from movies."

Kage made a face at the remark before they rejoined Capp and Star at the truck. While Capp filled the truck with fuel, Kage told them about Toby. He told them how wrong it had felt to do that to a teenager, but how it had also made him realize they needed something other than melee weapons and firearms. He felt knives would be better for close quarters or times when being silent was essential, pointing out Danterford's had a sporting goods department complete with hunting knives. None of them disagreed with him, but they were quick to voice concerns, the two main ones being the zombies that had started to gather outside the front of the store and the heavy steel doors rolled down over the glass entry doors of the store, indicating either the store had been closed at the time of the outbreak or people had shut themselves in. If it had been closed, the doors would certainly be locked, and if people had shut themselves in, the doors would probably be locked with the added danger of the chance they weren't very friendly people or they were zombies.

Kickz had been listening from inside the truck and decided to join them to offer his thoughts. "You have valid concerns, ja, but perhaps it is a risk worth taking. Yes, the hope is to make it to Phoenix where we will find it to be safe and free of the horrors we've seen over the past two days, but we can't rely strictly on hope. We must be realistic and prepare for the worst. Other than knives, we need to stock up on ammo, food, and water among other supplies. The store has all of it. We're already way behind the schedule we set for ourselves, we might as well gather the supplies and spend the night in there. We all need a rest, it looks secure, and it must be more comfortable than this truck. If we're lucky, any of the afflicted lurking around out here will give up by morning like they did at the warehouse."

They hadn't noticed Chris, Amber, and Jordan had gotten out of the truck until Chris spoke. "We think he's right. Phoenix may be safe, or it may be worse than Roma. We have to plan for all possibilities and take advantage of opportunities to get what we need when they present themselves."

"We all know they've got a point," Capp asserted. "Big stores like this usually have some sort of roof access to make it easier for maintenance to reach heating and cooling units. If we can get up there, we should be able to get inside. Only question is, how do we get up there?"

Kage pointed to the outdoor garden center at the end of the building. "The roof is lower there than the rest. If we back the truck up to it, we can climb up from the top of the truck."

"But from there to the main roof is too tall to make it up," Star noted.

"We're starting to draw a crowd," Gray warned, motioning to several zombies steadily moving toward them. "We need to make a decision pretty fast."

Kage had an idea. "Two of us in the cab, the rest on top of the truck with the pooch. We ease the truck over there, and if it looks like we can get from the lower roof to the main roof, we back the truck up, those on top cover the two in the cab while they get on top, then we all hit the roof. If it doesn't look like we can make it to the main roof, we carefully drive away and find a location safe for everyone to get back into the truck. We reevaluate from there."

"It's a start," Star sighed.

Kickz and Capp returned to the cab of the truck while the others retrieved Tooter who was in his carrier, closed the back of the truck, and climbed to the top of the box truck. Kickz slowly and carefully navigated the truck closer to the store, then along the end of the building by the garden center. Once they were closer, those on top of the truck could see a ladder running up to the main roof from the garden center roof. Kage lowered himself onto his belly, leaned down to the driver's side window, and told Kickz what they'd seen. Kickz expertly backed the truck up to the garden center fence, and he and Capp scrambled to the top of the truck. Amber was about to climb over onto the "roof" of the outdoor area of the garden center, which was nothing more than chain link fencing stretched tight over a metal grid, but Star pulled her back.

"Let me make sure it will hold first," he told her. To his surprise, she simply thanked him with no arguments.

Star carefully placed a foot onto the roof, being sure to step on one of the cross sections of the grid. It felt flimsy and swayed slightly when he put weight on it. He stepped up. With both feet and his full weight on the grid, he gingerly took one step forward then another, always making sure he stayed on the grid. He was holding his breath, but after a few steps, deduced the grid should hold. "It's not the most stable thing in the world, but it should be alright," he told the others. "Let me get across, and you guys come over one at a time. Stay on the grid."

Once to the ladder, he stood on the bottom rung and motioned Amber over. Amber stepped onto the grid and had Gray hand Tooter's carrier to her. Star thought it was admirable she wanted to get the little dog to safety but wished she'd left it to Gray or one of the others. He'd made a promise he intended to keep, whether she liked it or not, and he didn't want her to lose her balance because of the carrier. Amber made it almost halfway across when Tooter began to bark. Amber tried to calm him by shushing him and speaking to him softly, but he only grew louder. Knowing he would draw unwanted attention, she threw caution to the wind and ran to Star who stepped back down and ushered her up the ladder where Tooter continued to bark. Star climbed up behind them and motioned for someone else to cross.

Chris was the next to cross soon followed by Gray, Kage, and Capp. Tooter had quieted, but the damage was done. Zombies had indeed heard his barks and were congregating around the truck and the fence surrounding the garden center. Kickz told Jordan to go next. Jordan put one foot on the grid & froze. He felt the grid sway under his foot as he stared at the plants and racks below him. The zombies pushed on the fence as well as the truck causing him to feel both the grid and the truck rock beneath him. It utterly terrified him.

Kickz knew getting across that grid was the difference between life and death for both of them, but he could see something was very wrong with Jordan. "Jordan, are you afraid of heights?"

Jordan slowly nodded. He blinked hard, desperately trying to return his blurry vision to normal. Beads of sweat rolled down his temples. He felt as if he might pass out, and his legs felt like jelly.

Kickz took his arm to steady him. "We'll do it together." He knew it was dangerous but also knew Jordan couldn't do it alone.

Kickz stood behind Jordan, putting his hand on his back to comfort and steady him as well as nudge him forward. Jordan took the first step onto the grid and quickly took another with Kickz right behind him. Slowly but surely, they made their way across as more zombies gathered below and pressed on the fence. Suddenly the grid shifted violently, throwing Kickz and Jordan onto the fencing stretched over the grid.

"You've got to move now," Kage yelled from the main roof.

They struggled to their feet and bolted to the ladder. Jordan went up first, and as Kickz made it to the top, the grid shifted again but did stay standing.

"You okay," Kickz asked Jordan.

"I think so. Thank you for not leaving me."

"Over here," Gray called from the opposite end of the roof. He'd found a hatch covering a ladder going down into the building.

Climbing down the ladder, each of them wondered what might be waiting for them at the bottom. The ladder took them to a maintenance shop. After sweeping the shop and finding it to be clear, they poked air holes in a large box, sat Tooter's carrier in it, and covered the box with towels and moving blankets they found in the room. The goal was to ensure his safety and muffle any barking he might do while they cleared the building. With Tooter secured, they left the shop, closed the door behind them, and stacked boxes in front of it as an added measure of security for the small pup.

They then split into teams of two, each searching a different area of the building.

Jordan and Chris discovered the manager's office and heard movement behind its closed door. Earlier Star had discovered none of the siblings had any weapons other than pipes and had armed each of them with a pistol and ammo. The brothers readied those pistols and opened the office door. Their expectation had been to find survivors or perhaps one or two zombies in the office, but reality exceeded their expectation as five zombies shambled out of the small office. The brothers opened fire, quickly dispatching them. Chris and Jordan stepped over the corpses and into the office. Jordan looked behind the desk and found a writhing torso with nothing more than its head left attached, its eyes staring up at him. It was clear its arms and legs had been chewed off.

"That's so wrong," Jordan muttered before putting the creature out of its misery.

Kickz and Kage found a female zombie in a bathroom. "That's it! I'm going to stay out of bathrooms from now on," Kickz quipped.

Capp and Gray dealt with two zombies in the deli, and while Star and Amber didn't find any zombies, they did find a loading bay big enough to accommodate the box truck.

After they'd made a few more sweeps of the store

to be certain the building was completely clear, they all met back at the maintenance shop. Star told the others about the loading bay, and it was decided they would gather the supplies they needed, stack them in the loading bay, and if the zombies had dispersed during the time that took, they would move the truck into the bay. Guns, knives, and ammo were gathered from sporting goods. Food, drinks, and bottled waters were gathered from grocery, and manual can openers, disposable cups, plastic utensils, and paper plates were gathered from housewares. Other essentials gathered were things such as paper towels, toilet paper, washcloths, bath towels, soaps, and shampoos. After the gathered supplies were stored in the loading bay, Gray retrieved Tooter from the maintenance shop, and Kickz and Kage went back to the roof to investigate the situation near the truck. Most of the zombies had lost interest and wandered off leaving only a handful remaining.

"Suppose we should consider ourselves lucky they have a short attention span," Kickz giggled.

The remaining zombies presented Kickz and Kage an opportunity to put their new knives to the test. They quickly ascertained a well-placed blade through the eye, up the nose, into the ear, or, if the blade was long enough, through the bottom of the chin made short work of the creatures without any real noise to speak of. It only took them a few minutes to handle the zombies. Afterward, they pulled the truck around to the loading bay where Gray rolled the door up and closed it once the truck was safely inside.

After loading the truck with the supplies they'd already gathered, they decided it best to take full advantage of the store by gathering any other things they felt they might have occasion to use. Capp hit the hardware and automotive departments where he picked up tools, gas cans, oil, and anything he believed would be useful if the truck broke down or they found themselves forced to travel farther than planned. Kage went back to sporting goods to grab a camping stove, tents, sleeping bags, camping cookware, hunting bows, and arrows. Kickz gathered flashlights, batteries, candles, and matches. Chris and Jordan went after pillows, blankets, and changes of clothing for everyone while Gray made sure to stock up on dog food and treats.

Meanwhile, Star and Amber went to the pharmacy. Star was filling a box with bandages, peroxide, rubbing alcohol, thermometers, antibiotics, and various medications when he noticed Amber had slipped off. He found her in the feminine hygiene aisle putting several boxes of tampons and sanitary napkins into a shopping cart. He blushed when she saw him watching.

Amber held up a box of tampons. "I knew none of

you walking testosterone bags would think of these, and apocalypse or no, they are necessity for some of us."

When Star and Amber returned to the loading bay with the shopping cart, the others eyed it strangely. Star promptly plucked a box of tampons from the cart, held it up, and proudly announced, "Hey, testosterone bags, these are necessity for some."

It was Amber's turn to blush, and she laughed despite herself.

Kage suggested they might have use for the cart later and they should load the whole thing onto the truck. As they did, Chris, Jordan, and Gray entered the bay. Each of them was pushing a dolly with large boxes on them.

"What are those," Capp inquired.

Gray patted the top of his box. "Mattress in a box. We found a lot of them in a storeroom. The way we see it, we don't know when we'll get to sleep in a real bed again or even on something comfortable therefore, we're not going to pass it up when we can. We're going back to get five more."

Amber smiled. "Good thinking. Along that same train of thought, there's a stove and a fryer in the deli, I'll cook us a real meal."

All of them found the prospects of comfortable beds and a hot meal very appealing and were more than happy to help. Kickz offered to help get the mattresses, Kage volunteered to gather wine and wine glasses, and Star and Capp volunteered to help Amber in whatever way they could.

"Tomorrow we'll deal with the afflicted and the end of the world. Tonight, we'll enjoy the little things," Kickz triumphantly declared.

In the deli, Amber was surprised to discover Star knew his way around the kitchen. Seeing her shock, he explained his love of cooking and that he was taking culinary courses.

"If I'd known that I never would have volunteered to cook," she teased. "New plan, master chef. You cook, and I'll be your sous chef."

Capp watched the two of them and occasionally fetched ingredients they needed. He was glad to see Star relaxed and smiling, but he knew beneath that smile the perfect storm was brewing. Capp firmly believed a person could not kill another human being without some sort of emotional ramifications unless they were a sociopath. War taught him that lesson long ago. Watching the two young people had another affect Capp hadn't expected, he found himself looking at them and thinking of his own two children. Would his son have been like Star at that age? Would he have gone to college or followed in his dad's footsteps? If he'd gone to college, what would he have gotten his degree in? What about his daughter? Would she grow up to be as strong-willed and feisty as Amber? Would she like to cook? Was she safe? Was she scared? Was she alone? Was she even still alive? He knew as far as his son was concerned he'd never have answers to his questions, but he hoped it wasn't too late to get answers about his daughter.

Amber, Star, and Capp sipped wine and chatted about things having nothing to do with the hell they were existing in. It was pleasant and afforded them a chance to get to know one another. Star felt that was essential given there was a very real chance they might be the only people left alive. They were putting the food into serving dishes when Kage and Jordan appeared in the doorway.

"We have a surprise," Jordan beamed.

Kage and Jordan helped them take the food to the loading bay where tables and chairs had been set up complete with real dinnerware, tablecloths, linen napkins, and candlelight. A short distance from the tables were bean bag chairs positioned in front of a large television with a Blu-ray player hooked up. A stack of movies sat next to the Blu-ray player. A few feet from the television was a row of mattresses, one for each of them, decked out with bedding and pillows. Tooter was laying in the middle of one of them, happily chewing a rawhide treat.

Amber flashed the first truly genuine smile they'd seen from her. "This is amazing!"

Kickz stepped forward. "We decided if the three of you were going to prepare a gourmet meal for us the least we could do was provide a nice space to enjoy it."

"We also thought it might be a while before we have a normal night again, and we have earned at least one more night of normal," Kage added.

They ate, drank, and talked like old friends. Kickz watched and listened intently. It filled him with joy, but he wondered how they could seem so close considering most of them hadn't even known each other prior to two days beforehand. He supposed traumatic events such as they'd experienced could cause bonds to form quickly. He honestly didn't care what had created that bond as long as it was created. He very much viewed the group in the same way he viewed gamers, as an underestimated and undervalued community that had to have each other's backs, get along, and form friendships in order to continue to exist.

While Kickz observed the group as a whole, Gray observed one particular member of the group, Jordan. He'd noticed there was something different about the young man. Physically he was a man, he was the same age as Star, but something about him seemed far younger and rather innocent. On the other hand, there was an air of intelligence and wisdom about him. The boy was a bundle of contradictions, but something about him made Gray feel protective of him.

At one point during the meal Kickz asked the three siblings to do just as the others had done at the warehouse and tell everyone about themselves. Kickz explained the reasoning behind it, and Kage, hoping to make it less awkward for them, suggested each of the others repeat their stories for the siblings first. One by one each of the original five told their story. When it was Capp's turn he freely talked about his wife and children, which shocked Kage. He gave Capp a warm smile that clearly conveyed his approval and support.

Chris was the first of the siblings to share a little information about himself. "Well, my name is Chris Yant, and I don't make videos or stream, but I do play games. My tag is CJ Shockwave. Me and my brother and sister came here from Tennessee for the convention. I'm twenty-four, I work in a factory, and I love to make music and write songs. I'm the oldest of the kids, but I don't have any kids of my own. I've been in love with the same girl since I was sixteen, but it's kind of complicated so, technically, I'm single."

Jordan decided he would follow his brother. "I'm Jordan Yant, and like my brother, I'm a gamer, but I don't stream or make videos although I have thought about it. My tag is LilJ. I'm twenty with no kids, and I've had a few girlfriends but nothing serious. I had some dead-end jobs, but recently I started looking into college. I am the youngest brother, and like my brother said, I'm from Tennessee."

"Suppose it's my turn," Amber nervously observed. "My name is Amber Yant, and I am a twenty-two-year-old bartender from Tennessee. Pay sucks, but tips make up for it. I don't have any kids, and well, y'all know my relationship status. I love to sing despite the fact I'm not very good at it. Like my brothers, I don't make videos or stream. Unlike my brothers, I don't even play any games so, no tag. Heck, I only came on this trip to spend time with my brothers."

Kage asked Chris and Jordan if they played on PC or console. Upon the brothers answering with console, the others looked at one another with knowing smiles, and Chris picked up on it instantly.

"Uh-oh, PC master race alert," Chris groaned.

"Nothing like that," Kage assured him. "Yes, we're all PC players, but I promise you, we're not going to pull the master race crap. Personally, I never understood why players from both sides look down on each other. We're all parts of the same beast."

“Exactly,” Kickz agreed. “And I swear to all of you, those afflicted out there do not care if you play on PC or console. We all taste the same to them.”

“Why do you call them afflicted,” Jordan puzzled.

“To me, calling them zombies is almost disrespectful,” Kickz answered. “With the exception of Amber, we all play games, and we’ve all seen and probably played zombie games. I’m sure Amber has watched zombie movies. Games and movies portray them as soulless monsters to be destroyed. Ja, to be sure, we must destroy them to survive, but at one point they were just like us. They didn’t choose to become what they are; it isn’t their fault. They’re victims of something beyond their control, just the same as someone afflicted with cancer or something of the like.”

No one spoke for several moments as the impact of his words hit them like a truck.

Finally, Star decided the mood needed to be lightened. “I have one question. What are we going to do about this non-gamer amongst us,” he asked as he cast a playful gaze in Amber’s direction.

Amber grimaced at him. “Is it a crime to not be a gamer?’

“No,” Gray responded, “but it’s abnormal and probably should be a crime.”

The group laughed and began to speculate

about what Amber's gaming name should be. Star's suggestion, SassyLass, won the popular vote.

"Okay, okay," Amber said, rising from her seat. "Now that you've christened me, let's watch a movie." She strolled over to the stack of movies and looked through them. One movie stopped her in her tracks. She turned back to the group with an exasperated glare. "Really, people? Whose idea was this?"

"What is it," Star asked.

She held up the movie. "*Night of the Living Dead.* Seriously?"

They roared with laughter.

While the others slept, Kickz stood watch. He was sitting on one of the bean bags with a pistol on his lap, watching a movie, and eating popcorn when Capp got out of bed.

"Got enough popcorn to share," Capp asked.

"Of course. Pull up a bean bag."

Capp eased down onto one of the bean bags. "What ya watching?"

"Some sort of vampire movie. Not a very good one either."

Capp snorted. "Better than a zombie flick."

Kickz eyed Capp. "Why aren't you sleeping?"

"Worried about Phoenix. What if we're wrong? What if it's not secure? What if this is happening all over the state or even the country? Phoenix is three times the size of Roma, imagine what we saw in Roma multiplied by three."

Kickz wiped the popcorn salt from his hands on a napkin. "I won't tell you not to worry because I've wondered the same things. We'd be fools to not consider all of that, but what other options do we have?"

"We have to give it a try, there's no question about that, but we need a backup plan." Capp pointed to the others sleeping soundly. "Some of them are awfully young. Why put them in even more danger by taking them to Phoenix until we know what we're facing?"

"What do you suggest?"

"We're only a couple of hours outside of Phoenix. I say we take one of those cars outside and go scout it out. This place is secure and has everything they need. I saw handheld CBs in sporting goods. We take one with us, leave one here with them, and radio back whatever we find. If Phoenix is safe, we'll come back for them. If it's not, we'll come back here and hole up until we figure out our next move."

Kickz was hesitant to split up the group, but he had to admit Capp made a compelling argument. "You may be on to something. We should try to get one of the smaller cars started. It will be much easier to maneuver around obstacles, especially if a hasty retreat is called for. You get the

CBs ready, and I'll throw some things into a couple of backpacks."

Before they left Kickz wrote a note to explain to the others what they were doing and to tell them to keep the CB on. He left both the CB and the note on the table.

"Shouldn't we wake one of them up and tell them," Capp suggested.

"No, they'd only insist on going with us. Let them rest."

CHAPTER 6

"What the hell," Kage yelled, his booming voice waking everyone else.

Gray shot out of bed in a panic. "What is it? What happened?"

"They're gone," Kage exclaimed, thrusting Kickz's note at him. "Kickz and Capp are gone!"

"They left us," Star asked in shock. "They're good guys, they wouldn't do that."

Gray handed Star the note. "They did it because they are good guys."

"What does that mean," Chris asked.

"Probably better for you to read it yourself," Gray told him. "I think you'll understand it better that way. I'm horrible at explaining things."

While Chris, Amber, and Jordan read the note over Star's shoulder, Gray pulled Kage to the side. "I know this isn't what we'd planned, but if you'll calm down and think it over, you'll see they're trying to do the right thing. It's not like they left us high and dry.

We have everything we need here, and this place is pretty safe. We'll be fine."

"I know that," Kage snapped. "I'm not worried about us; I'm worried about them. What chance do two people have on their own in Phoenix if it has been overrun?"

The CB crackled. "Gray? Kage? Star? Are any of you there," Kickz asked.

Kage rushed to pick up the radio. "Oh, we're here alright, and at least one of us is pissed! What were you thinking?"

It was Capp's voice that responded. "We'll be fine, buddy."

"Who says I'm worried about whether or not you're fine?"

Capp's voice was filled with amusement. "I know you, Kage."

Kickz informed them that he and Capp were just approaching Phoenix. He said the roads were littered with debris and abandoned cars, just as they'd seen in Roma, but in Phoenix's case, the lanes going into the city were completely clogged while the lanes out were almost clear. Star theorized it might have been because other people thought, as they had, Phoenix would have been secured. Kickz tried to relay as much of what he was seeing as possible while Capp drove. He reported many afflicted wandering between the abandoned cars and along the roadsides. Some afflicted were making a meal of a deer, and smoke was billowing into the sky from some areas of the city, which didn't bode well for what they'd find.

Driving through the city streets it was painfully obvious the capital city of Arizona had not been spared the fate that had befallen Roma. Some buildings looked as if they'd exploded, and others had afflicted clawing at their windows from the inside. Bodies and pieces of bodies were on the sidewalks and in the streets. Car and store alarms echoed throughout the city as afflicted roamed freely. Phoenix had fallen.

"It's gone," Kickz somberly radioed back to the others. "I'm so sorry."

Capp turned the car around, pointing it back toward Danterford's and the rest of the group. A line of afflicted followed behind them, but they couldn't keep up with the car. On the way out of town, Kickz noticed something he hadn't on the way in.

Kickz pointed to a small road to the right. "Turn down there," he told Capp.

Capp didn't question it as he'd come to understand Kickz didn't do anything without a good reason. Turning into the end of the road he saw what must have caught Kickz's attention. It was a sign indicating there was a Danterford's Mega Center somewhere in the vicinity. It was only a moment before it came into view.

"If you're thinking of getting more supplies, we can get a little in this car but not much," Capp advised.

"That's not what I'm thinking. Stop right here. Don't get too close."

Danterford's Mega Centers were complete one-stop shopping for just about anything one could need or want. While Danterford's Emporiums were impressive, the Mega Centers offered everything the Emporiums did and more, including a restaurant, lumber and building supplies, an automotive repair shop, and a full-blown gun shop. They also housed Danterford's Wholesale Distribution warehouses. Danterford's had been the target of two activist groups for a couple of years. One blamed the company for the downfall of countless mom and pop businesses, and the other thought Danterford's didn't pay their employees a living wage. Both groups had vandalized several of the chain's locations, forcing the company to up their security measures, such as installing fences around all their Mega Centers since they were normally favorite targets of the groups. The fences were composed of waist-high concrete topped by five-foot-tall, heavy gauged, steel fencing. With its fence, the massive building looked like a fortress.

"Kickz, what are you thinking?"

"You were military. Admittedly, I know very little about the U.S. military, but it stands to reason the first place the military would be sent to contain a situation or extract survivors would be any government facilities or locations, such as capital cities. Am I right?"

Capp nodded. "A lot of factors figure into that, but yes, that would likely be the highest priority, but Kickz, we just saw containment failed."

"True, but when the dust settles, they'll come back to search for survivors and access damage, no?"

"They probably will."

"Then wouldn't it make more sense to be near the capital city rather than in a little town in the middle of nowhere," Kickz asked.

"I think I see where you're going with this."

"We could survive for a very long time with everything in there, and surely, we wouldn't need to for that long because the government will send the military back out in a couple of weeks tops. Why don't we spend that time safe behind that fence?"

"Let's go grab up everybody else."

Capp and Kickz made good time on the way back to the rest of the group. They parked the car in front of Danterford's and ran around back to the loading bay door, dodging a few afflicted along the way. Kickz used the CB to tell Gray to open the door.

"You guys ready to roll," Kickz excitedly asked once inside.

Star was bewildered. "I thought Phoenix was out of the question."

"It is, but it isn't," Capp answered.

"Stop talking in code," Kage huffed. "What have you two cooked up?"

Capp hurriedly explained the plan and the line of reasoning behind it. "If we leave right now, we can make it there before dark."

"Does it have a shower," Amber half joked.

"Actually, it does," Capp happily informed her. "Danterford's provides free showers at their Mega Centers for their truck drivers."

Amber hopped to her feet. "I'm in. Let's go, boys!"

Chris watched his sister with amusement. "Bossy much?"

Star laughed. "You heard the lady. Let's move out, gentlemen!"

Kickz and Chris took the box truck while the others took the car.

Amber stared out the car window. "You would think there would be somebody somewhere. I keep expecting to pass someone."

Jordan gasped when they pulled up to the Danterford's Mega Center. "My God! It's freaking huge!"

They were all pleased to see there were no

afflicted outside the fence nor inside the fence. There were only three cars in the parking lot, and the gates were secured with a chain and padlock. The group took all those things as good indicators the store was probably clear.

"This is too easy," Gray observed, his tone conveying the nervousness he was feeling.

"It looks like they were closed when all the hell broke loose, but I thought the Mega Centers were open seven days a week," Kage offered.

Chris was feeling as anxious as Gray was. "Don't they usually stay open late," he asked.

"You're both right," Gray answered. "So, why were they closed? None of it makes sense."

Kage sighed. "We can drive ourselves crazy trying to figure it out, or we can decide to not look a gift horse in the mouth. I'll get the crowbar and take care of that lock and chain."

Once the truck and car were parked safely inside the fence, the group's first order of business was to make certain the store was in fact clear. The Mega Center took longer to sweep then the previous store had, but to their delight, they only found three afflicted inside, all of them were employees. Once they'd dispatched the afflicted, Gray, Chris, and Kickz took them outside the fence for a proper burial while the rest of the group set about other tasks. Kage and Star gathered supplies to secure the gate and obstruct the view through the fence. Jordan,

Amber, and Capp unloaded the truck. While they felt safe behind the fence, they all worked swiftly because they still didn't want to be outside after dark. The sun had just begun to set when they finished up and made their way into the store for the night.

Knowing everyone was starving, Amber rushed off to the restaurant kitchen in search of something to feed them all. Jordan accompanied her, followed by Tooter who'd taken a liking to the young man. Chris and Kickz set about making a map of the locations of each door and labeling where they led. In the process, they made sure all exterior doors were secured. Gray and Kage walked through the building making notes of where light switches and windows were while Capp and Star searched for backup generators.

"How long do you think we'll be here," Star inquired of Capp as they walked.

Capp had serious doubts there would ever be any rescue for them. His military experience told him the chances were very slim, but he didn't want to admit that to anyone just yet. "Hard to tell without knowing what shape the rest of the country is in," he lied.

"Do you think it happened all over the country?"

"Not sure, but I wouldn't rule it out."

"I wonder if my parents are okay," Star

murmured almost to himself.

"I think we've all got somebody we're worrying about. It's natural, and it's torture."

"Thinking about your daughter?"

"Yeah. Yes, I am," Capp admitted.

"I want you to know, I was sorry to hear about your wife and baby. I didn't know them, heck, I didn't even know you when it happened, but the loss of someone you love is a tragedy for anyone, especially the loss of a child. You're pretty tough to still be standing after that."

Capp could hear the sincerity in Star's voice, and it meant more to him than he could find the words to express. "It was rough, and afterward there was a time I wasn't standing. You know, there are lots of things in life that can knock us down when we thought we were strong enough to keep standing. Losing people we love, war, and being forced to do something against our nature are just a few things that can bring us to our knees."

Star sensed they were no longer talking about Capp. "I'm fine."

"You probably are fine right now, but sooner or later, it is going to hit you. When it does, it will hit you hard, and if you hold it in, it will tear you apart. It will shred you from the inside out. I don't want you to let that happen. When it hits you, I'm here."

Star was uncertain of what he should say or even wanted to say. He appreciated what Capp was attempting to do for him, but he wanted nothing more than to just forget about it. “Thanks,” he mumbled.

CHAPTER 7

As he so often did, Kickz sat alone in the tower. Per usual, he wondered what was taking them so long. It had been months, where were they? He looked at the picture in his hand. The faces of his wife and son smiled up at him. Were they safe? Would he ever see them again? He knew his only hope of a reunion with them was a military rescue. Again, he wondered where the military was and what was taking them so long.

He heard moaning below him. Looking down, he saw another afflicted clawing at the fence. It seemed more had been showing up lately. Why were they leaving the city? Would they ever rot away? The afflicted's moans were abruptly drowned out by another sound that caught Kickz's attention. He turned to look in the direction the sound came from. Was he dreaming? His eyes had to be playing tricks on him.

He squinted hard then squeezed his eyes shut tight, but when he opened them, the vehicle was still there, drawing ever closer. With the speed of a marathon runner, he made his way down from the tower.

Kage met him at the bottom. “Kickz, did you see that? Is that really a car? Should we open the gate?”

“I’m not certain we should, but we’re going to!”

Mere seconds after the gate was opened, a SUV sped through it. Excited yet cautious, Kage and Kickz kept their hands on their pistols. The SUV came to a stop, and both the front driver’s and passenger’s doors opened. A man and woman stepped out.

The man extended his hand. “Hi! I’m Dragon, and this is Welsh. I believe we saw you in the city yesterday.”

Kage warily shook his hand as Kickz shook Welsh’s. “So, that was you,” Kage asked.

“Sorry about that,” Welsh apologized. “We didn’t know who you were or if you could be trusted.”

Kage glared at the new pair. “We were on a scouting mission for any signs of survivors or the military returning. We couldn’t have done anything to make you feel you couldn’t trust us.”

“If you were unsure of trusting us, why are you here now,” Kickz asked flatly. “What changed between yesterday and today?"

Dragon smiled. "We found out we have some mutual friends."

Both back doors on the SUV opened. Two men, a woman, and a young boy got out. Kickz gasped at the sight of them, and Kage saw the color drain from his face.

"Kickz, bro, what's wrong," Kage asked.

Kickz didn't respond to his friend or even acknowledge he'd heard him. He ran to the woman and boy and wrapped his arms around them. Tears streamed down his face, but he was smiling. The woman and boy, also crying, returned his hug. Dragon, Welsh, and the two men looked on with smiles. Kage was completely confused until the boy uttered one word that explained it all.

"Dad," the boy cried.

"I thought I'd never see you again. "How is this possible," Kickz asked though tears of joy.

Kickz's wife pointed to the two men who'd gotten out with them. "They helped us."

One of the men stepped forward. "Hello, Kickz. That's Mike, and I'm JC."

Rise Survivors

Games4Kickz- G4K has quickly become a beloved personality in the world of gaming content and streaming. His unique accent, a blend of German and Irish, combined with his own language, "Kickzism", is hard to resist. His positive energy and genuine love for what he does makes each of his videos and broadcasts a great experience. Holy ballz, what a treat!
YouTube: @Games4Kickz
Twitter: @Games4Kickz

Kage848- A truly nice guy, Kage's friendly personality, snarky sense of humor, and ability to thoroughly explain the games he plays has made him a favorite with viewers. While Kage is normally a laid back kinda guy, occasionally something riles him up, and at that point his viewers may be treated to the Kage Rage, an endearing characteristic to many of his viewers. You should go watch Kage for days!
YouTube: @Kage848
Twitter: @Kage848

Starsnipe- Starsnipe is a shining example of what the younger generation can do. A full-time college student who still makes time for his family, Star's upbeat brand of gaming has made him popular with viewers of all ages. From his kind wishes for everyone to his ability to remain positive

while kicking zombie butt makes him living proof there is something good to be found in both gamers and the youth of today. Now, have a fan-freakin-tastic day, but take an umbrella, there's a slight chance of shotgun rain.
YouTube: @Starsnipe
Twitter: @Starsnipe1

J.C.'s Channel- JC should consider a career in writing. His love of the game combined with his ability to create and voice his own storylines has made him a favorite among viewers. Watching JC is like watching a good television show. Add his great personality to the mix, and he has a lot of people DOOOOOOMED to binge watch. Mike, pass the popcorn.
YouTube: @JCsChannel
Twitch: https://www.twitch.tv/jc_lc
Twitter: @JC_Channel

Capp00- Capp's even, mild mannered tone is in stark contrast to his adventurous nature in-game. His willingness to try anything for the sake of the game has made him a hit with viewers. With his trusty sidekick, Sylvia, Capp will try any stunt that he and even viewers can think up. His tests are always entertaining and educational. Sylvia tested, Capp approved.
Youtube: @capp00
Twitch: https://www.twitch.tv/capp00
Twitter: @Capp00

GrayGhostZoro- Gray may be new to the world of making videos and streaming, but he's a veteran when it comes

to gaming. He's always had a love for the game in all its many forms, and now he uses it to get to know more people in the gaming community on a personal level. Friendly and a little goofy at times, this southern goofball is one to watch. Hauntingly entertaining.
YouTube: @GrayGhostZoro
Twitch: www.twitch.tv/grayghost_zoro
Twitter: @GrayGhost_Zoro

About the Author

Mandy was born in middle Tennessee along the Alabama border, an area rich in history & storytelling. From the time she could talk, Mandy loved nothing more than telling stories which naturally progressed into her love of writing. At a young age she was lucky enough to have the privilege of meeting the late, great author, Gregory Mcdonald whose inspiration & influence she carries with her to this day.

Mandy is a proud mother & grandmother. She resides in Virginia with her husband, Michael, & their family of fur babies.There's more to tell, but she'd much rather tell you herself. Listed below are a number of ways to hear it straight from the horse's mouth.

Bluesky: @mandycmoore.bsky.social

Instagram and Threads: @mandyc_moore

Website: cmstarscreations.com

YouTube: @CMStars_Creations

Mandy Collins-Moore

Discord and Other Links: linktr.ee/cmstarscreations

CM STARS CREATIONS SUPPORTERS & FRIENDS

While there have been so many who have supported me, Gray, and CM Stars Creations, and we appreciate them all, there have been some who have been there since the very beginning or gone above and beyond anything we could have hoped for. I just wanted to take a moment to acknowledge them and thank them. To those folks I say thank you from the bottom of my heart, and I can't wait to see what we do together in the future!

Love,
Mandy

Brandon Connors

Lori Miller

Miss Jamie

SummerofKorn

Blue Haines

Aultra

www.ingramcontent.com/pod-product-compliance
Lightning Source LLC
LaVergne TN
LVHW091009080826
845145LV00003B/1187

* 9 7 8 1 9 6 9 4 6 8 0 0 1 *